Sweet Obsession

NIGHTS SERIES BOOK FOUR

A.M. SALINGER

COPYRIGHT

Sweet Obsession (Nights Series Book 4)
Copyright © 2018 by A.M. Salinger
All rights reserved.
Registered with the US Copyright Office.
Second paperback edition: 2024
ISBN: 978-1-9996184-3-8

www.AMSalinger.com
shop.adstarrling.com

Edited by www.ElfwerksEditing.com
Cover Design by A.M. Salinger

BOOKS BY A.M. SALINGER

NIGHTS

One Night - 1

The Escort - 2

Tokyo Heat - 3

Sweet Obsession - 4

Sweet Possession - 5

The Proposition - 6

Undisclosed - 7

Hush - 8

One Day - 9

Nights Series Short Story Collection

TWILIGHT FALLS

Alex - 1

Carter - 2

Hunter - 3

Wyatt - 4

Drake - 5

Tristan - 6

Miles - 7

CHAPTER ONE

THIS ASSHOLE!

Ash Colby scowled at his watch. He took a shallow breath, uncrossed his legs, and propped his elbows on his knees. The motion brought pain surging across his temples. The migraine had been with him for the last two hours. Although he would have loved to blame it on the humidity of Singapore's late September monsoon season, Ash knew his current circumstances had led to the headache jackhammering against his skull. The fact that he'd just gotten off a seventeen-hour flight from San Francisco wasn't helping either.

Ash rubbed a hand across the back of his neck before glaring at the secretary seated behind the modern walnut desk to his left.

"He knows I'm waiting, right?" Ash snapped.

John Peace sighed and nudged his smart, black-rimmed specs up his nose.

"Yes, Ash. Luke is aware that you've been waiting a while."

"Forty fucking minutes is not a while, John," Ash said between gritted teeth.

"Language, Ash," the secretary murmured.

Ash looked around the chic marble and wood waiting room overlooking a panoramic vista of the dazzling city and sun-kissed bay beyond the glass wall behind the secretary's desk.

"There's no one else here."

John ignored Ash's acerbic observation and studied him steadily.

"You look a bit peaky. Would you like some water?"

Ash scowled. He knew the secretary was only trying to be helpful, but he was past caring at this point.

"No, I don't want fucking water, John. I want to know why my lord and master has summoned me all the way here from Stanford five days before term starts."

Ash couldn't help grind his teeth as he recalled the terse phone conversation from two days ago. The motion exacerbated the band of tension gripping his head and raised his ire further.

"Luke would like to see you," John had said coolly when he'd called Ash at eight on a Sunday morning.

Ash frowned as he walked through the front door of his condo. He dropped his gym bag on a chair and headed to his bedroom.

"What's this about, John?" he said, irritated. He sat on the edge of the bed, kicked off his shoes, and fell backward onto the sheets. "And when did he get back to San Francisco?"

John hesitated. "He isn't in San Francisco."

Ash blinked at the ceiling before slowly sitting up, his incredulity quickly turning to anger.

"Wait a minute. You're telling me Luke is in Singapore and he wants me to go there to see him? Fuck no!" he growled.

John sighed. "This is important, Ash. You know Luke wouldn't make such a request unless it was an urgent matter."

Ash rubbed a hand across his eyes and swallowed hard. There was no denying the truth in the secretary's words.

Luke Rutherford, Ash's former guardian and the current custodian of his rather substantial trust fund, was not a fickle man.

Ash inhaled shakily and tried to quell his rising temper. "Can you at least tell me what this is—"

Someone took the phone from John.

Ash froze when Luke came on the line.

"A car is coming to pick you up in thirty minutes. Pack a bag and be ready. The jet's already at the airport."

Ash stared blindly ahead as the line suddenly went dead. He listened to the dial tone for a stunned moment before flinging the phone across the room and throwing himself back on the bed. A cry of rage left Ash's lips as he raked his hands through his hair. Despite the fury and frustration burning in his veins at Luke's outrageous command, Ash could not help the shudder of awareness that raced through him after hearing Luke's voice.

It had been over a year since they last spoke.

For one insane moment, Ash considered not obeying the man who quite literally owned him, body and soul. The man he had been in love with for as long as he could remember.

The man who had broken his heart and shattered his dreams five years ago, on the night of Ash's seventeenth birthday.

The thought of the possible reprisals Luke would visit upon him if he did not get on that plane sent a quiver of apprehension through Ash. The guy was capable of anything. Just as Luke had promised, the car arrived promptly at eight thirty and Ash lifted off from San Francisco International Airport an hour later.

Ash sighed, his thoughts returning to his current predicament as he leaned back on the expensive Barcelona chair and propped his feet on the coffee table. He ignored John's disapproving stare and indicated the walnut door opposite from where he sat with a jerk of his head.

"So, who does he have in there? Must be someone damn important if he's ignoring me for this long." Ash paused. "Not that the asshole doesn't ignore me on a regular basis anyway."

John pinched the bridge of his nose. "I would really appreciate it if you didn't keep calling Luke an asshole, Ash. And, yes, he's got his asset manager in with him right now. Mr. Sorvino flew in from Tokyo yesterday and is heading straight to Japan after their meeting."

"Yippee for Mr. Sorvino," Ash muttered. "Lucky bastard. I hope I'm back on the jet tonight as well."

John hesitated. He opened his mouth and closed it soundlessly.

A tendril of unease shot through Ash as he stared at the secretary's face. He narrowed his eyes. "What?"

"Nothing," John murmured.

Ash was still studying him suspiciously when Luke's door opened. A man walked out of the office.

The stranger was tall and dark, with a commanding presence that had as much to do with his handsome face and his arresting gunmetal eyes as it did with his incredibly ripped body. Had Ash not been unreservedly in love with Luke, he would have found the guy captivating.

A figure appeared behind the asset manager. Ash's mouth went dry when Luke stepped out of the room.

At six foot two, Luke Rutherford's hard bodied, toned frame more than matched the man beside him. With dark hair that most women would kill to sink their hands into, finely trimmed stubble that framed a strong, angular jaw, and amber eyes that had the power to silence a crowded room, Luke Rutherford was not only sinfully attractive, he was also the embodiment of a successful businessman and billionaire.

Ash swallowed.

Sexy fucker.

CHAPTER TWO

LLUKE BARELY SPARED ASH A GLANCE AS HE HELD OUT A hand to the asset manager.

"It was great to see you, Cam. And I'm sorry you had to come all this way to do this."

Ash blinked, surprised. It wasn't every day he heard Luke apologize to anyone.

Cam Sorvino shook Luke's hand. "Not at all. I had stuff to do in the Singapore branch of the firm anyway, so this trip killed two birds with one stone."

Luke leaned against the doorframe, folded his arms across his chest, and crossed his long legs.

Ash stared.

The two men standing close to each other made for a remarkable combination. Even John couldn't help but gaze at them unblinkingly.

"When's the big day?" Luke said. He cocked his head at the fund manager's left hand.

Ash noted the white gold and platinum band on Cam's ring finger for the first time.

Cam grinned.

"Gabe and I haven't picked a date yet. He's working on this place right now, a new luxury resort in Hawaii. He says it's gonna be stunning. They don't normally do weddings, but we're thinking of asking the guy who owns it if we can get married there anyway." He arched an eyebrow. "I'll be sure to invite you."

Luke smiled faintly. "That would be fun."

Ash almost fell off the chair. He didn't think he'd seen Luke Rutherford have anything remotely resembling fun in over half a decade.

His startled movement drew the two men's gazes. Amber eyes narrowed as they focused on him, sending his pulse skittering.

"I don't believe you've met my former ward," Luke muttered. "This is Ash Colby, heir to the Colby Corporation. Ash, this is Cam Sorvino, my fund manager."

Cam's eyes widened slightly as Ash rose to his feet. He exchanged a guarded glance with Luke before crossing the waiting room and shaking Ash's hand.

"It's nice to finally meet you."

Ash mumbled a greeting, curious about the secretive look the two men had just traded.

"Your car is waiting downstairs, Mr. Sorvino," John said. "And there's a message from a Mr. Cavendish. He said that if you don't get your ass back to Tokyo in time for your own birthday, Mr. Skye and Madame Claude will—and I quote— 'Get Gabe onstage at *Saron* and help him do a striptease.'"

Cam groaned. "Those assholes."

Luke cocked an eyebrow. "I didn't know it was your birthday."

"I'm not exactly a child anxiously waiting for cake and gifts, Luke," Cam said breezily as he headed for the exit. "Although I wouldn't mind one particular blue-eyed gift," he added under his breath.

"You want to borrow the jet?" Luke called out.

"Thanks, but no!" Cam yelled as he entered the lift.

Silence descended on the waiting room when the elevator doors dinged closed. Luke nailed Ash with an inscrutable stare before turning on his heels and heading back into his office.

Ash gazed at the open doorway, apprehension crawling across his skin despite his smoldering anger. He didn't know why he felt like he was about to walk into the lion's den. He crossed the floor and entered the room, the sound of the door closing behind him a death knell to his ears.

❦

WHAT THE FUCK IS THIS KID EATING? MIRACLE-GRO?

Luke adjusted his suit and sat behind the dark wood and Italian white laminate executive desk, grateful for the partition that hid his growing erection from view. Ash strolled in and plonked himself down on the couch opposite him. He narrowed his steel-blue eyes at Luke, not bothering to hide his resentment.

It had been over a year since Luke had last seen Ash in the flesh. The young man had shot up another two inches in that time. He'd also filled out in all the right places, his athletic physique toned to perfection while his brown hair shone with sun-kissed highlights from his time in California.

Perfect face, perfect body, perfect legs, perfect ass.

Luke's gaze strayed briefly to Ash's full lips. He swallowed a groan.

And a perfect, cocky, sexy mouth I would kill to have swallow my dick.

That last thought sobered him up.

Although Luke wanted nothing more than to strip the angry young man seated across from him, bend his delicious body over his desk, and fuck him until neither of them could walk, it was the one thing he would never do. The one promise he could never break.

He didn't deserve to lay a single finger on Ash Colby. Not after what he had done. Not even if he'd loved him since the day he was born and been in love with him for over half a decade.

"Care to tell me why the hell you had me flown halfway across the world?" Ash said without preamble.

Luke winced internally. He deserved that. He took a deep breath and assumed the cold demeanor he usually displayed when he was with Ash, steeling himself for what was about to go down. It was a carefully cultivated facade, one he had adopted to create and maintain the distance between them.

It was the only way Luke could protect Ash from his carnal urges.

"As of right now, you are no longer a graduate student at Stanford. I've enrolled you in the architectural design program at the university here, in Singapore. You'll also be living with me."

ASH BLINKED. HIS HEART STARTED AN ERRATIC POUNDING in his chest as deathly silence descended on the room. He stared at Luke, hoping and waiting for the *Fooled you!*

The man opposite him studied him coolly, golden eyes unblinking. That was when Ash realized Luke wasn't joking. Ash froze for a dizzying moment, disbelief warring with rage inside him. Rage won. Ash jumped to his feet and stormed to the desk.

"*Are you out of your fucking mind?!*" he barked.

"My mind has never been any clearer," Luke replied steadily. "Your personal items are being packed as we speak and will be flown to our home here in the next twenty-four hours." He paused. "Your Stanford supervisor was obviously sad to see you go but understood your sudden change in circumstances. He gave you a glowing recommendation. And I'm selling your condo in Los Altos."

Blood roared in Ash's ears as he glared at the man opposite him, too stunned to speak. Hatred surged through him, the feeling so visceral he couldn't help but dig his nails into his palms. He found his voice a moment later.

"Why are you doing this?" Ash asked hoarsely.

Something flashed in Luke's eyes then. Something

Ash had seen only once before in his life. Fury. A rage so deep, it seemed to turn the man before him to stone.

Ash's stomach twisted, the pain knifing through him so great he wanted to throw up.

Oh God! He really hates me, doesn't he?

Ash swallowed past the sudden lump in his throat, wondering for the thousandth time what he had done to deserve Luke's anger.

"You owe me an answer, Luke. You can't just ignore me for five years, then barge back into my life and pretend you want to play house."

Luke propped his elbows on the armrests of his leather executive chair and dropped his chin on the back of his interlocked hands.

"What if I told you this was for your own good?" he said quietly.

CHAPTER THREE

Luke sensed the second Ash lost it. The steel-blue eyes that haunted his dreams flared before darkening to the color of a stormy sea.

Ash marched around the desk and grabbed the front of Luke's shirt.

"How old do you think I am?" he snarled. "I'm not a child, Luke, so if you've got something to say, say it *goddamn it!*"

Luke's gaze dropped from the gorgeous, angry face hovering less than a foot from his to the fingers grasping his shirt, his pulse drumming a wild beat in his veins.

Ash was too close. Way too close.

"Let go," Luke said stiffly.

Ash blinked, self-awareness dawning in his eyes for a second. It was replaced by incandescent fury in the next instant.

"I won't," he grated out. "Not until you tell me what this is really—"

LUKE MOVED SO FAST, ASH COULD ONLY GASP. HE SHOT to his feet and crowded Ash against the desk, one powerful knee roughly parting Ash's legs. Luke stepped inside the cradle of Ash's thighs and used his brawny frame to force Ash backward over the desk.

Ash instinctively gripped Luke's hips with his knees as he lost his balance. His elbows hit the white laminate surface behind him, sending stationary scattering to the floor. Luke leaned down and braced his hands on either side of Ash's head, his stance intimidating, his face a scant few inches from Ash's. They both froze, amber gaze locked on blue, their breathing loud and ragged in the sudden stillness.

Heat flooded Ash's cheeks when he registered their intimate position. Despite the anger simmering inside his heart, he couldn't stop the thrill of desire that coursed through him.

Jesus, he smells good!

The feel of Luke's muscular frame against him, the scalding hotness of his body through his thousand-dollar suit, the warmth of his breath as it washed over Ash's skin, the golden flecks in the eyes above him—Ash absorbed it all, knowing he would never get this close to the man he loved ever again.

Something shifted in Luke's eyes. Ash stared, his heart racing against his ribs, not quite sure what he was reading in Luke's darkening expression. Heat flamed Ash's ears in the next moment when he felt Luke's erection press against his thigh.

Ash's dick twitched. His gaze dropped to Luke's mouth before he let out a shaky breath.

⚜

SHIT.

The breathy little sound Ash had just made shot straight to Luke's groin and sent his pulse spiking.

Ash licked his lips nervously and stared at Luke's mouth. Luke swallowed a curse. He wanted nothing more right now than to press his own lips to Ash's delicious Cupid's bow. To part Ash's plump curves and dip inside. To explore Ash's cocky tongue with his own and taste him in the most intimate way.

Luke sobered when he saw the flush of color painting Ash's cheekbones and ears. He masked a grimace, straightened, and shifted his rock-hard dick from the taut flesh of Ash's inner thigh.

Ash blinked, an odd mixture of relief and disappointment flashing across his face. He flattened his hands on the desk and started to rise as Luke stepped away from him.

"Ouch!"

Luke startled at Ash's muttered exclamation. He looked down and saw the cut on Ash's hand where he'd pressed his palm against the sharp end of a stapler.

"Damn it, be careful!" Luke said gruffly.

He pulled Ash up until he sat on the edge of the desk, grabbed his hand, and kissed the small wound. Heat shot through Luke when the salty sweet taste of

Ash's skin and the coppery tang of his blood hit his tongue.

Ash went deathly still, shock widening his pupils.

Luke stiffened.

Fuck.

He couldn't believe he'd just done what he used to do all those years ago, when Ash was still a child.

It was a ritual they'd instigated from the very first time Ash started to walk. Whenever Ash took a tumble, whenever he scraped a knee or grazed an elbow, he would always run to Luke first and present his wound for him to kiss it better, much to the amused dismay of Ash's parents and the delight of Luke's own father and mother.

Although the age difference between them spanned over a decade, Luke had always treated Ash like the little brother he'd never had and the rite of soothing Ash's battle injuries was one Luke had cherished until the young Colby heir entered his teens and outgrew it. They had remained close, their attachment to each other untouched by distance even after Luke started traveling the world in his new role as one of the CEOs of his family's business.

Until that fateful day six years ago, when their entire world had come crashing down around them.

ASH REGISTERED THE EXACT MOMENT LUKE SHUT him out.

He was amazed he was even thinking coherently at

this point, so overwhelmed was he at the sinfully sensual feel of Luke's lips and tongue against his skin. It had been well over a decade since Luke had last kissed him this way.

Luke released Ash's hand and walked stiffly around his desk to the glass wall overlooking the glistening waters of Marina Bay. He raked his fingers through his hair and let out a frustrated sigh, the lines of his shoulders rigid while he gazed outside.

"I'm sorry," Luke murmured after a short silence.

Ash blinked, still frozen on the edge of the desk. He shifted his feet to the floor and stood staring at Luke on shaky legs, his brain struggling to process what had just happened.

Including the shocking fact that the man he loved had been gloriously hard for him.

Luke finally turned and looked at Ash, his face cast in shadows by the bright light behind him. "I'll get the car to take you home."

A sliver of the anger that had burned through Ash a minute ago surged inside him once more, dampening the frisson of excitement running through him.

"You still haven't answered my question, Luke," Ash said in a hard voice.

Luke hesitated. "We'll talk. Tonight."

CHAPTER FOUR

ASH STARED AT THE LUXURIOUS CONCRETE AND GLASS mansion before him.

Luke's home was located in a secluded area of Sentosa Island, half an hour from Marina Bay. Dusk had started to fall by the time the chauffeur guided the car through a set of imposing electronic security gates and onto a drive spiraling up through thick woodland.

Lights became visible between the trees after some five hundred feet and the land started to open out. The house finally appeared around a curve, a white geometric construction spread out over one level on the summit of a rise, with a two-story block jutting out at one end.

As an architectural design major, Ash could tell how much passion and thought had gone into creating this place.

The car slowed and stopped in a courtyard fringed by manicured lawns and lush vegetation. Ash got out and shrugged his backpack on his shoulder, eyes roaming admiringly over the stunning building while the driver took his travel case out of the boot.

The thick walnut door fronting the property swung open on silent hinges. A petite woman stepped out. She was dressed in a pink kebaya—a traditional Indonesian outfit—and looked to be about fifty.

"Mr. Colby, it is nice to finally meet you," she said, pressing the palms of her hands together and bowing.

Ash emulated her greeting.

"You must be Xin Yi," he murmured to Luke's housekeeper.

The woman smiled. "Just call me Xin. Please follow me."

Ash thanked Luke's chauffeur and headed after the housekeeper. He stepped inside a beautiful hallway dominated by a solid ebony floor and paused to take in the mansion's remarkable interior.

The building opened up before him, an artfully conceived design of whitewashed concrete walls and wood partitions that created an illusion of modern rooms within what was effectively one giant, open-plan space. Glass walls with sliding doors spanned the north-facing aspect of the home and overlooked a patio and sundeck enclosing a swimming pool running half the length of the mansion. A short expanse of manicured lawn edged by tropical fruit trees gave way to thick woodland. The landscape artist who'd designed the gardens had evidently wanted to preserve as much of the natural terrain as possible.

Ash studied the eclectic decor as the housekeeper showed him around before leading him to his room.

The mansion was vastly different from Luke's home in San Francisco—or more precisely, the ancestral home of the Rutherfords.

Descendants of wealthy Scottish migrants who had come to the US in the nineteenth century, the Rutherfords had amassed a vast fortune after investing in the myriad of businesses that had flourished during the American Industrial Revolution, establishing a dynasty that continued to grow over the next two centuries. By the time Luke—the last Rutherford heir—was born, the Rutherfords' fortune was estimated to be over ten billion.

In comparison, Ash's family, the Colbys, were relatively nouveau riche, with a construction empire that spanned only two generations.

Luke and Ash's fathers had been firm friends since their college days. When the Colby Corporation moved its headquarters to San Francisco, Charles and Susan Colby bought the mansion next to William and Judith Rutherford. The two families grew even closer after that, the arrival of Ash shortly after Luke turned fourteen completing their tight-knit unit.

Ash had only wonderful memories of his childhood and growing up with Luke. It wasn't until he entered puberty and had his first wet dream that he realized his feelings for Luke were changing. The adoration and hero worship he'd held for Luke over the years had slowly transformed into a different kind of love, one that confused and enthralled Ash in equal measures while Luke's brotherly affection toward him remained unchanged. Ash became more reserved in Luke's company after that, although he hardly saw the younger Rutherford during his mid-teens. Luke was away a lot, traveling the world and immersing himself in the business he would eventually inherit. The jealousy that speared through Ash whenever he overheard tidbits of gossip about the numerous actresses and models the Rutherford heir bedded during that time only reaffirmed his growing obsession with Luke.

No one had known then that the day Luke would take over his father's mantle would come sooner than either Luke or Ash had expected.

"Dinner will be ready in fifteen minutes," Xin said, bringing him back to the present. She bowed in the doorway of his room and started to walk off.

"Will Luke be home by then?" Ash said distractedly, his gaze riveted to the picture frame on the nightstand next to the beautiful, king-size rosewood bed dominating the floor.

Xin turned around. "Mr. Rutherford said he will be late today. He told me to serve you first."

Ash frowned as Xin disappeared in the direction of the state-of-the-art kitchen.

I thought he wanted to talk.

He pursed his lips, headed over to the bed, and picked up the black-and-white photo.

It showed the Rutherfords and the Colbys together at one of their notorious summer barbecues, their faces full of joy and laughter as they posed for the camera.

Pain twisted through Ash when the memory of that day washed over him. He'd been thirteen at the time and had just started to realize that he liked Luke. He put the picture frame down, unpacked the meager change of clothing he'd brought, and placed his toiletries in the marble bathroom.

&a.

BY THE TIME ASH FINISHED THE SPLENDID THREE-COURSE meal Xin had prepared and watched the housekeeper putter down the drive on her Vespa on the way to her home, the anger that had filled him when Luke made his astounding proclamation in his office a few hours ago had returned with a vengeance, as had his headache.

Ash paced the mansion as he waited for Luke to return, his temper growing with each passing minute. When ten o'clock came and went, he headed behind the bar, poured himself a double Scotch, and plopped down on one of the deck chairs by the pool.

A modicum of peace settled over Ash as the fiery liquid burned his throat. He stared up at the dazzling night sky, the spirit slowly numbing his mind and his senses while he listened to the faint rustle of leaves in the trees hedging the lawn and the hum and buzz of insects.

Ash's cheeks warmed when he recalled Luke's arousal during the incident in his office. *Was it anger that brought him to that state? And what about the way he kissed the wound on my hand, like he used to do when I was a kid? Does it mean he doesn't hate me, like I think he does? If so, why did he have that look of rage on his face when I asked him why he was forcing me to relocate to Singapore?*

Ash closed his eyes and tried to shut out the hundred thoughts clouding his brain, too exhausted to try to analyze the mystery that was Luke Rutherford. A wave of drowsiness suddenly washed over him. Ash startled. He sat up and put the glass down on the deck.

The Scotch had been a bad idea. He wasn't used to drinking and the spirit was making him woozy. He patted his cheeks roughly. He needed to be awake and in full control of his mind when Luke returned.

A warm breeze blew through the garden and sent ripples skittering across the surface of the swimming pool. Ash eyed the crystal-clear green water. He hadn't expected that he'd be staying the night in Singapore or that he'd have the chance for a swim. He hesitated.

Fuck it. It doesn't look like that asshole is coming home anytime soon.

CHAPTER FIVE

Luke sighed as the car headed up the drive to the mansion. It was nearly eleven at night and he'd just left the office.

The events of this afternoon played through his mind once more. Luke had anticipated that seeing Ash again would be a challenge, one he knew he would have to grit his teeth and overcome if the urgent strategy he'd had to come up with in the last week was to work. That things hadn't panned out exactly the way Luke had wanted them to didn't totally come as a surprise.

Ash was the one person in the world who could completely derail his normally unflappable mind and his ironclad intentions. Luke had thought that time away from the young man would dampen the forbidden attraction he felt for him.

He was wrong.

His body's instant and visceral reaction to Ash when he saw him waiting outside his office had stunned Luke. And the insane desire Luke had felt when he trapped the young man against his desk and felt his body heat was more intense than it had ever been before, more potent than anything Luke had ever felt for *anyone* before. Luke had wanted to taste Ash badly. To take him. To mark him. Luke had wanted to sink his teeth and his cock into Ash's flesh and brand his body with his scent and his insides with his seed.

But it wasn't what had almost happened right there on his desk that had doused Luke's ardor as effectively as a bucket of icy water. It was the expression on Ash's face that had finally made Luke come to his senses and end the intoxicatingly dangerous situation they'd found themselves in.

Luke didn't think he'd mistaken the desire in Ash's steel-blue eyes. That shocking awareness had stayed with him for the rest of that day, making it hard for him to concentrate. He'd wondered numerous times if he was losing his mind or if Ash had wanted him to kiss him as badly as Luke had wanted to.

Luke's absentmindedness hadn't escaped his secretary.

"Are you going to tell him the truth?" John had asked before he left for the day.

It had been past seven that evening. Although Luke didn't like keeping his staff late, he knew John didn't mind. The guy had been his aide and a friend for over five years, and Luke paid him more than generously for his dedication to Rutherford Industries and to him.

"Should I?" Luke had asked tiredly, raking a hand

through his hair where he sat, trying to focus on several convoluted documents.

John had pulled a face.

"Ash is twenty-two, Luke. And the kid is smart. I know having the backing of the Rutherford name didn't hurt his application to Stanford or the university here, but they wouldn't have accepted him if he wasn't a brilliant student."

"That's the problem, John." Luke rubbed his eyes. "To me, he'll always be that little kid. The one whose diapers I once changed and whose scrapes I used to bandage."

John had watched him for a silent moment.

"Well, you'd better come to terms with it and quick," he'd stated in a cool voice. "You might not feel ready to tell him the whole truth yet, but you're going to have to give him something to justify why you've just turned his entire world upside down by forcibly moving him across the world to another country."

John's words replayed in Luke's mind as the car pulled up in the courtyard and the chauffeur got out to open his door.

"Seven thirty a.m. as usual, Mr. Rutherford?" the man murmured as Luke stepped out.

"I'll probably drive to the office tomorrow, Dan," Luke replied, trying to mask the weariness in his voice. "I'll call if Ash and I need you."

A small thrill ran through Luke as he said those words. *Ash and I* had an unexpectedly sweet connotation to it, one that made his heart swell with joy briefly.

The chauffeur nodded and climbed back inside the limo. Luke stood and watched the vehicle's taillights disappear around the bend, aware he was stalling. He turned toward the mansion. There were still lights on inside. Luke braced himself and headed in.

Silence greeted him when he entered the hallway.

"Ash?" Luke called out.

He dropped his bag on a console table and stared down the corridor that led to Ash's bedroom. Motion up ahead caught his eyes. Tiny waves disturbed the surface of the pool at the rear of the property. Luke headed into the lounge, fingers tugging at the knot in his tie, gaze seeking the man outside through the open glass doors.

Ash bobbed in the water as he reached the end of the swimming pool.

Luke froze in the next moment, his breath stilling on his lips.

Holy. Fuck.

The words he had been rehearsing all through the evening, the tone he should adopt to talk to Ash, the way he should react to the young man's predictable anger—everything Luke had been planning fled his mind when Ash climbed out of the pool naked.

Ash rose to his feet and stood staring out over the garden with his back to Luke. He raised his hands and slicked the wet dark locks flush to his scalp, the water running in rivulets down his neck and back.

Luke's cock stirred and swelled as he took in the exquisite, sculptured lines of Ash's body. It was clear that Ash worked out regularly. The underwater lighting and the lamps framing the deck and garden cast soft light on his beautiful muscles and the toned, honey skin of his shoulders, back, and legs.

Luke's erection grew to full mast when his gaze narrowed in on the ravishing curves of Ash's firm ass. The urge to sink his teeth into those two perfect globes of tight flesh swept over Luke like a storm.

Sweet Je—

Luke swallowed a curse when Ash turned. The young man headed to the deck chair where he'd left his clothes and shoes, oblivious to Luke having a mini coronary in the lounge. As if the sight of Ash's sinfully sweet behind hadn't been bad enough, the full-frontal view just about killed Luke.

Ash's dick had grown splendidly from the time Luke last recalled seeing it when he changed Ash's diapers and when Ash used to run naked around the Rutherfords' swimming pool as a toddler. Add to that his defined six-pack and the flat, taut muscles of his lower belly, and Luke wondered if he was going to stroke out from all the blood rushing from his head to his own cock.

Ash froze when he finally registered Luke's presence. Much to Luke's chagrin, he gasped and held his clothes protectively in front of his groin.

"You're late!" Ash snapped.

Here we go.

Luke suppressed a grimace of pain at his rock-hard erection, dreading the difficult conversation ahead.

"I'm sorry," he murmured. "I got sidetracked by a thing at work."

That the *thing* was standing in front of him right now wasn't something Luke was about to admit to Ash.

Ash crossed the deck and entered the lounge, his expression still hostile.

"You eaten yet?"

Luke blinked at the unexpected question. "No."

Ash mumbled something rude under his breath.

"Why don't you shower and change?" he said stiffly. "I'll warm up dinner."

CHAPTER SIX

ASH'S HEART THUDDED RAPIDLY AGAINST HIS RIBS. HE masked his growing arousal behind the bundle of clothes in his hands and headed swiftly past Luke, dripping water all over the floor.

The feel of Luke's hot stare on his naked body had raised goose bumps on Ash's skin. A feverish feeling filled Ash's chest, making it hard to breathe as he nearly ran for the safety of his bedroom. He dropped his clothes on the bathroom floor and showered rapidly before changing into his pajamas. Luckily, he'd brought a pair.

Ash headed to the kitchen and had just finished rewarming a plateful of food in the microwave when quiet footsteps sounded behind him. He stiffened and turned in time to see Luke pad barefoot into the kitchen. The Rutherford heir had changed into gray sweatpants and a white T-shirt that hugged his muscular chest and broad shoulders. His dark hair still glistened with water, the smell wafting off him so intoxicating Ash nearly groaned out loud.

Ash set the plate of steaming food on the marble island.

"Thanks," Luke murmured, climbing onto a barstool.

Ash narrowed his eyes. "And you'd better finish all those vegetables."

Luke blinked. His lips curved in an amused smile, causing heat to flood Ash's cheeks. It was the same threat Luke had used when Ash was being fussy with his food as a child.

Ash turned and opened the fridge, his pulse racing at their strangely domestic situation. He eyed the drinks rack inside critically before glancing at the well-stocked wine cooler across the room.

"What do you want to drink?" he tossed at Luke over his shoulder, his tone coming out sharper than he'd intended.

"Water's fine," Luke said.

Ash grabbed a cold bottle for each of them and ate an apple while Luke dug into his meal, an oddly companionable silence settling over them.

It wasn't until Luke pushed his plate away and drank the last of his water that tension started winding through Ash once more.

"So, you finally gonna tell me what the hell this is all about?" Ash said, not bothering to hide the anger in his voice.

Luke propped his elbows on the marble top and

rubbed his hands down his face, his expression suddenly weary.

"What if I said I just wanted you here, by my side?"

Ash's heart stuttered. He leaned against the island on the opposite side of where Luke sat, his legs suddenly shaky and his ears ringing with Luke's shocking admission.

The wild hope blooming inside Ash's chest faltered and died when he registered the calculating look in Luke's eyes. Fury and sorrow filled him in equal measure in the next instant.

"I'd say, stop being a fucking asshole and tell me the goddamn truth!" Ash growled.

Luke stifled a sigh. He was quiet for a long time, his gaze hooded as he studied Ash.

"They're back," Luke said finally.

Ash's train of thought stumbled to an abrupt halt.

"Who's back?" he asked, puzzled.

A muscle jumped in Luke's jawline.

"Your aunt and uncle."

Ash felt the air rush out of him. This time, he gripped the edge of the island with white-knuckled fingers while a wave of painful memories washed over him.

Fuck.

Shortly after Luke had turned thirty and a month after Ash's sixteenth birthday, both their parents had lost their lives in a tragic car accident close to their homes. The woman who had smashed into the Rutherfords car and pushed it over the edge of the cliff spanning the Pacific coastline, instantly killing the two couples inside, was three times over the blood alcohol level limit when the police arrested her.

As if losing his parents hadn't been bad enough, what had happened at their funeral drove Ash deeper into the spiral of darkness that his life had become overnight. Catherine Bernardino, Charles Colby's estranged sister, had emerged from the woodwork with her husband Peter at her side and declared she would take custody of Ash. Ash hadn't known much about his aunt apart from the fact that his father hadn't trusted her and she'd been disowned by the senior Colbys when she was twenty-five. He couldn't even remember what she looked like, having met her only once when he was three years old.

As they'd had no close relatives they would have willingly entrusted their only child to, Charles and Susan Colby had named Luke's parents in their will as Ash's legal guardians if something were to happen to them. With both his parents and his guardians deceased, the court had refused to award custody to Luke despite the hard battle the heir and newly appointed head of Rutherford Industries fought in court. The fact that Luke was single, had no blood relation to Ash, and had a high-powered career with enormous responsibilities that took him all over the world meant he was regarded as an unsuitable candidate to look after Ash's needs.

That Ash's own wishes hadn't been taken into account by the family court judge was something that still enraged him to this day.

Ash had disliked his aunt and uncle from the

moment they moved into his family home. Even though he had only been a teenager at the time, he'd sensed they were not interested in his welfare and had their eyes on the substantial trust fund his parents had set up for him in the eventuality of their deaths and which now held all the frozen assets of the Colby Corporation. A trust fund he would only get access to when he turned twenty-five and which would be managed by Luke and Rutherford Industries until that time.

Ash had almost been relieved when his aunt and uncle sent him off to boarding school, his only sorrow being the fact that he would see Luke even less from that time on. That Catherine and Peter had been squandering the generous allowance Luke had allocated to them for Ash's maintenance was something Ash never reported to the Rutherford heir.

Ash had stuck his head down and concentrated on his studies, the friends he made at his new school keeping him sane while the despair of being separated from Luke ate at his heart and soul. Only one thing had kept Ash from completely losing it during that time.

The hope that he and Luke would be together again, in the future.

Ash's dream stayed strong and true until that fateful day five years ago. The day he turned seventeen. The day his aunt summoned him back home, telling him she had a surprise in store for him for his birthday.

The day he saw Luke have sex with his aunt and uncle.

CHAPTER SEVEN

Luke's heart twisted as he watched the blood drain from Ash's face.

God, I hate this!

Rage flooded Luke at the thought of Catherine and Peter Bernardino. The same rage that had burned through him for the last week and that had ignited all those years ago, when he'd discovered Ash's aunt and uncle had been planning to get rid of the young Colby heir so as to lay claim to his trust fund.

Luke had been suspicious of Catherine from the moment he'd laid eyes on her. It was evident that Catherine had worn the pants in the couple's relationship and Peter mostly tagged along, doing as he was told. But it wasn't until the private investigators Luke had hired to look into their past uncovered their gambling history and the exorbitant debt they owed a Las Vegas loan shark that Luke's suspicion turned to dread.

Even though Luke had hated being separated from

Ash, he'd been relieved when the couple had sent the kid off to a boarding school a couple of hundred miles away. Luke had kept on issuing the monthly upkeep for Ash's care, knowing full well the Bernardinos were spending most of it on themselves, and had a PI firm keep a close tab on the couple at all times to gather evidence against them.

It was the only reason they'd uncovered the Bernardinos' scheme.

When the PI firm reported that Catherine and Peter had started visiting a legal accounting firm with a dubious reputation, Luke realized the couple were looking at ways to ensure they could get their hands on Ash's trust fund. With no other living relative left in the world, the only way the assets of the Colby Corporation would revert to Ash's remaining next of kin was if something happened to the teenager. It was a state of affairs that had shocked Luke when the Rutherford Industries' lawyers confirmed this fact to him. Although Luke had immediately started the legal proceedings to change the terms of Ash's trust fund, he had known it would be a long and protracted affair and his fear for what could happen to Ash in the interim had grown.

So Luke had approached Catherine and Peter with an offer they couldn't refuse, one his lawyers had vehemently warned him against. They'd eventually given in to his wishes and drawn up the contract Luke had presented to Ash's aunt and uncle.

"I know what you're up to," Luke had said coldly when he'd confronted the couple in the Colby family home. He'd thrown the papers and photographs the PI firm had taken of them leaving the legal accounting firm in their faces.

Peter had panicked when he'd seen the pictures. Luke had barely looked at him, his gaze focused on Catherine's cruel blue stare.

"So what?" she said icily after a short silence. "You haven't got proof that we've done anything wrong."

"Read the rest of those papers," Luke said between gritted teeth.

Catherine's eyes widened when she looked over the contract Luke's lawyers had put together. She paled when she saw the final sum of money mentioned.

"You're buying us off?" she said hoarsely.

"Yes," Luke snapped. "I want you out of here and out of Ash's life for good."

Catherine and Peter pored over the paperwork while Luke waited, mouth dry and heart thundering inside his chest.

"The Colby Trust Fund is worth more than this," Catherine finally said with a condescending smile. "We'd be fools to accept this paltry sum."

Luke swallowed his fury at her words. *This bitch!*

"It's all you two are ever going to get, so you'd better take it and run," Luke bit out. "My lawyers are working on changing the terms of the trust fund right now. By next week, you guys won't get a single cent if Ash dies," he added, the lie effortlessly leaving his lips.

Hate filled Catherine's eyes at that point.

"Babe, let's just take this and—" Peter mumbled.

Catherine held out a hand, stalling him. She studied

Luke for a long time, her blue gaze sending a shiver down his spine.

"Thank you for this offer, Luke. We will get back to you soon."

Luke's hands fisted at his sides as he stared at Ash's aunt. The fact that she was deliberately going to let him stew hardly came as a shock. She was a vile woman and the faster he got her and her husband out of Ash's affairs, the better.

And for that, I'd be willing to do anything.

That thought came to haunt Luke a few days later. On the night before Ash's seventeenth birthday, Catherine called him with a counteroffer that chilled him to the bones.

"Peter and I would be happy to accept the terms of your contract. On one condition."

Luke dug his nails into his palms as he waited, knowing Catherine's long pause was intentional.

"I want you to have sex with us," Catherine said calmly.

Luke froze then, his mouth opening and closing soundlessly for an instant.

"*What?*" he barked when he could speak again.

"Since you had us tailed, I'm sure you've discovered that Peter and I have some rather special…interests when it comes to our sex lives," Catherine said in a voice devoid of shame.

Luke ran a hand through his hair and stared out of his bedroom window toward the dark ocean pounding the shoreline at the bottom of the cliff. When the PI firm had reported the Bernardinos' visits to several notorious swingers and BDSM clubs in the San Francisco area, Luke had not been completely surprised. He'd seen the way Catherine looked at him over the last year and sensed her sexual interest despite her open hostility toward him.

The current situation no doubt thrilled her twisted soul.

"That's all you have to do, Luke," Catherine said in a saccharine tone. "Just have sex with us once and we'll sign this contract and be on our way."

Luke swallowed, his heart vacillating between hope and disgust. If he did as they asked, he didn't think he'd ever be able to face Ash again. And he suspected Catherine knew this too.

"So, what's it going to be, Mr. Rutherford?" Catherine asked, the glee in her voice so obvious Luke felt like tossing the phone right out the window.

"I'll do it," he finally whispered, a deep pain piercing through him.

"Tomorrow night. Nine o'clock. We'll be waiting upstairs in the bedroom."

CHAPTER EIGHT

L ΥΚΕ'S PULSE STUTTERED. "BUT IT'S—"

"Ash's birthday?" Catherine said sweetly. "Don't worry. He's spending it at boarding school."

Luke felt a part of himself die when she disconnected. He listened to the dial tone for a long time as he stared blindly into space, wondering if he was insane for having agreed to go ahead with this, knowing Catherine had deliberately picked tomorrow's date to further twist the knife already embedded in his heart.

Ash's face swam across his vision a second later.

Luke swallowed. *He's worth it. He's worth everything.* He closed his eyes. *It's just one time.*

Luke repeated that mantra the whole of that sleepless night and into the next day. He repeated it even as he headed into the Colby family home that evening and took the stairs to the bedroom that had once been Ash's parents. He repeated it when Catherine ordered him to sit, fully clothed, in an armchair and watch while she and Peter had sex in front of him. Repeated it even when she beckoned him to stand at the end of the bed, pulled his zipper down, and gave him a blow job.

Luke didn't think he could hate the woman any more than he already did until she looked up at him after a minute of trying to get him hard.

"Why don't you pretend I'm Ash?" she murmured coyly, her red-tipped fingers stroking his limp cock while she sucked his shaft.

Luke had frozen then, air locking in his throat as he stared down at her. Fury sent a red mist across his vision. He grabbed the back of Catherine's head and jerked her lips off his flesh.

"What did you just say?" Luke bit out.

Peter groaned where he pumped his dick in Catherine's body, Luke's action having obviously caused her to clench tightly around him. He came a second later, his animal grunts echoing around the bedroom, the mattress squeaking erratically beneath him.

Catherine moaned and licked her lips, her slutty gaze still on Luke's face.

"I've seen the way you look at him. Like you want to sink your dick into his ass." She smiled. "Just close your eyes and pretend I'm him. I'm sure you've fantasized about Ash blowing you when you've jerked off to the shitty kid before."

For one wild moment, Luke had wanted to hit her.

The thrill that flashed in Catherine's eyes when she read the expression on his face was what stayed Luke's hand. It would only satisfy her and he would no doubt live to regret his action. Catherine opened her mouth wide and took Luke deep inside her throat while Peter started jacking himself off behind her.

Luke curled his fingers in Catherine's hair and dropped his head back. He stared blindly at the ceiling, self-hatred and revulsion a quagmire threatening to drown him.

He's worth this.

So Luke closed his eyes and thought of Ash—the person he loved more than life itself, the one he was doing this for. Luke still couldn't pinpoint the exact moment he'd fallen for the boy he'd doted on all his life and who had worshipped him from the moment he could walk. The only thing Luke was certain of was that he had never before felt this burning desire for another human being, male or female, in his entire life.

And when he came in Catherine's mouth a moment later, Luke hoped and prayed the gaping wound in his heart would one day heal and that he'd be able to look the young man who'd always idolized him in the eye at some point in the future without bitter self-loathing and disgust.

TREMORS RAN THROUGH ASH'S BODY AS HE RECALLED what he'd seen in what had once been his parents' bedroom the night of his seventeenth birthday.

Ash had been surprised and more than a little suspicious when Catherine had told him she would be sending the car round to pick him up that evening. His misgivings had only grown when he'd entered the silent mansion and couldn't find her or his uncle.

It was the noise that drew Ash upstairs. An odd noise, one he hadn't heard before.

Shock tore through Ash when he came in view of the open door of the bedroom. He stood frozen for a moment at the sight of his aunt and uncle having sex and was about to turn and dash down the stairs when he heard Catherine call out to someone. Ash's feet moved of their own volition then, bringing him to an alcove to his right, the curtains hiding his presence while still giving him a full line of sight.

His heart almost stopped when he saw a figure appear at the end of the bed.

Ash stared dazedly at Luke, blood roaring in his ears and his pulse drumming so fast in his veins he thought he would faint, unable to grasp what it was he was witnessing. He watched as Catherine opened Luke's zipper and flushed when he saw her palm Luke's cock before kissing and licking it. Catherine worked Luke's dick for a minute before looking up and saying something to him.

The shocked expression that flashed across Luke's face and the rage that followed it as he grabbed Catherine's hair and yanked her head back branded itself in Ash's mind.

He had never seen Luke so angry before, as if he wanted to kill someone.

Catherine murmured something again. This time, Ash truly thought Luke would strike his aunt. Then, he dropped his head back and stared at the ceiling for a moment before closing his eyes and letting Catherine blow him, the tortured expression on his face so intense and vivid that it stayed there even as he climaxed in her mouth.

Ash didn't stay to watch what happened afterward. He stumbled out of the alcove, ran down the stairs, and managed to make it to the car before breaking down. The chauffeur panicked and asked if he should get Catherine when Ash started sobbing brokenly in the back of the limo.

"*No!*" Ash shouted vehemently in between hiccuping and catching his breath. "Just—just take me back!"

Ash spent the entire drive crying—so much so that by the time he reached the boarding school, his eyes looked like he'd been stung by bees. He crept into the bedroom he shared with a friend and spent the entire night staring at the ceiling above his bed, his mind racing with a thousand thoughts.

Though Ash was still a virgin, he'd heard of threesomes. He wondered then how long Luke and his aunt and uncle had been having sex. The thought of Luke being pleasured by the woman Ash loathed most in this world had sent bile rising in his throat. He'd rushed out of his bed, dashed into the bathroom, and thrown up in the toilet, his dry heaves echoing against the tiled walls for a long time.

He got the phone call from his lawyer the next morning.

Catherine and Peter Bernardino had renounced

custody of Ash and left the Colby estate. His new legal guardian until he turned eighteen would now be Luke Rutherford.

Ash waited then, for Luke to ask him to return home. When days passed and the call never came, he phoned Luke's private number and his office, only to get Luke's voice mail and the repeated message from Luke's secretary that he was traveling abroad for work and didn't want to be disturbed.

The chasm that grew between them over the weeks and months that followed, and Luke's cold behavior on the odd occasion when they met in person in the subsequent year slowly turned Ash's heart to ice, so much so that there were days when his hatred for the Rutherford heir almost matched his love for him.

Once Ash turned eighteen, Luke supported his application to Stanford, bought him a condo in Los Altos, and basically washed his hands of him. The next four years passed in a blur as Ash knuckled down and concentrated on his studies, his broken heart gnawing at him most days. A torment he knew time would not alleviate. A wound on his soul that would never heal.

CHAPTER NINE

LUKE WATCHED ASH DRAW A RAGGED BREATH AT THE news that his aunt and uncle were back in their lives.

"So?" Ash said.

Luke blinked. More than surprise at Ash's reaction, he was shocked at the fury in the young man's voice. Luke frowned.

"So, I don't want them anywhere near you."

Ash straightened, the expression on his face one Luke had never seen before.

"Why? I'm not a child and I'm no longer your ward," Ash said coolly. "What I do and whom I choose to do it with isn't any of your concern."

Although what Ash had just said was the truth and made perfect sense, Luke couldn't stop the disgruntled, possessive feeling that surged through him.

"They are not good for you, Ash," he said, scowling. "And I'm worried about what they might try and do to you this time around."

Ash inhaled sharply. His eyes narrowed in the next instant, suspicion shining brightly in the blue depths.

"What do you mean, *this* time around?"

Shit.

Luke nearly bit his tongue at his blunder. He wasn't ready to admit the truth to Ash. Not yet.

Ash folded his arms across his chest as an uncomfortable silence stretched between them. "Or is it that you just want them for yourself?" he said between gritted teeth. "After all, you three haven't fucked for like, what, five years?"

Luke's heart twisted painfully before starting a heavy pounding against his ribs, the sound of his world crashing down around him a distant roar in his ears.

"*What did you just say?*" he breathed.

Ash ran a trembling hand through his hair and squeezed his eyes shut, as if he couldn't bear to look at Luke's face anymore. When he blinked them open, the hurt and loathing in the steel-blue gaze pierced Luke's soul like a knife.

"I saw you. The night I turned seventeen. Catherine called me to the mansion. She said she had a surprise in store for me." Ash's voice broke for a moment before he let out a bitter chuckle. "I guess she just wanted to flaunt your sick relationship in front of me, right?"

Rage flooded Luke. He stumbled off the barstool and walked over to the sink, fingers biting into the ceramic edge as he stared blindly out of the glass wall overlooking the rear garden, the fury coursing through his veins so great it threatened to drown him.

"You weren't meant to be there," Luke said, agony slurring his voice as the devastating truth finally sank in. "She promised."

The terrible deception Catherine had inflicted on him five years ago suddenly made Luke want to vomit. But, more than her lies, more than the sick game she'd played with him, the fact that she'd deliberately called Ash to the mansion so that he could catch them in the act burned through Luke. He knew then that if he ever saw Catherine Bernardino in person again, he would likely strike her.

"Oh God. *I hate that bitch!*" Luke slammed his fist down on the marble top, his nails digging into his palm so hard he almost drew blood, the pain he'd inadvertently helped inflict on Ash a mistake he could never forgive himself for.

Ash's entire world tilted to a stop at Luke's words, his racing pulse skipping a beat. He widened his eyes.

Did I misread the situation that night?

Concern rushed through Ash in the next moment as Luke continued pounding the marble top with his fist, head bowed and shoulders shaking with rage while he ranted and cursed.

"Stop it," Ash whispered, his voice raw with anguish. He moved then, his feet carrying him to Luke's side, his hands rising to grab Luke's wrist as the latter brought it down to the countertop once more. "*Stop it!*"

Luke froze, his beautiful face contorted in a mask of hate and self-loathing as he stared blindly at Ash, his amber eyes glittering.

Just as the night of his seventeenth birthday, Ash felt his heart break all over again. He knew then that he'd gotten it horribly wrong. That what had happened five years ago wasn't as straightforward as he'd thought it was. That Luke hadn't been having an affair with his aunt and uncle. That there was more to it than a simple act of sex.

There was only one person in this world who could tell him the truth.

Ash took a shaky breath and pressed Luke's hand to his chest.

"Tell me, Luke," he whispered. "Tell me what happened that night."

LUKE'S BREATH CAUGHT IN HIS THROAT AT THE devastatingly haunting expression in Ash's eyes.

Ash's touch burned Luke's skin, his heart thudding erratically under Luke's fingers where they rested on his chest. The emotion blazing across Ash's face was so bittersweet that Luke felt the walls he'd built around his own aching heart start to shatter and crumble.

Ash didn't hate him. Despite what he'd witnessed the night of his seventeenth birthday, he didn't loathe him, like Luke so justly deserved. Instead, the devotion and fondness Ash used to express to Luke with every smile, every word, every move he made when they were together in the past radiated off him in waves, a balm that soothed Luke's fractured soul, a solace he thought he would never again find.

At that moment, Luke couldn't have loved Ash more. He swallowed as he came to the agonizing decision he'd hoped to put off for as long as he could.

I have to tell him the truth. I can't lie to him anymore.

Luke inhaled deeply and started talking.

Ash stilled when Luke told him what the PI firm had uncovered over the year the Bernardinos had custody of him. Ash's eyes flared after Luke confessed his fears for his safety and admitted to the crazy deal he'd asked his lawyers to put on paper so he could buy the Bernardinos off and get them out of Ash's life.

"How much?" Ash asked hoarsely after a stunned silence.

Luke blinked. "How much what?"

"How much did you give them?"

Luke hesitated. "Seven million."

Ash gasped. Fury twisted his face in the next instant. His fingers bit into Luke's hand.

"Those fucking assholes!" Ash hissed. He swallowed before taking a shaky breath. "And the sex?"

Luke closed his eyes briefly at Ash's tortured expression.

"It was the one condition they had," he confessed after a pause. "I—it was the only way I could get them out of your life."

Ash gazed at him steadily, anger and anguish warring on his face.

"So, you—you didn't enjoy it?"

Luke's pulse jumped at the brazen question. *"Hell no!"*

"But—," Ash hesitated, embarrassment painting red flags across his cheekbones, "—but you came in her mouth."

Luke stared, not quite believing they were actually having this conversation.

Despite the gravity of the situation, he couldn't help but be slightly turned on by the fact that he and Ash were talking about sex, nor could he quell the small burst of happiness that bolted through him at the blatant jealousy in Ash's eyes.

"She wouldn't have let me out of there otherwise," Luke said with a groan. "I only promised to watch and let her blow me. And, trust me, getting hard for that bitch wasn't easy."

Ash blinked rapidly.

"So, you didn't—" He trailed off awkwardly.

Luke's dick twitched at Ash's bashful expression. "No, I didn't fuck her."

Ash's gaze grew hooded.

"Were you thinking about your lover?" He released Luke's hand and took a step back before twisting on his heels. "Was it that model you were going out with at the time?"

Luke stared at the flush of color darkening Ash's nape, a deep sense of loss washing over him at the sudden break in their physical contact.

"No. I was thinking of the person I love."

The confession left Luke's lips before he could stop it. He froze, suddenly wishing he could take the words back.

CHAPTER TEN

ASH STIFFENED. HE FELT BLOOD DRAIN FROM HIS FACE AS he turned toward Luke once more, the shock of Luke's disclosure regarding what had happened all those years ago swept away by the agonizing pain that tore through him at his last words.

"The person you love?" Ash repeated shakily.

Luke remained silent, his expression growing shuttered.

Ash stared at him for a moment, knowing he wasn't going to say anymore on the matter. He took a ragged breath and raked a hand through his hair, his gaze dropping to the floor.

"I—anyway, I'm just glad you don't hate me," Ash mumbled after a short silence.

A gasp left Ash's lips when Luke closed the distance between them and grabbed his shoulders.

"*What?*" Luke barked. "Why the hell would you think that?"

Ash blinked, stunned at the biting strength of Luke's fingers and the despair pasted across his face.

"You never brought me home. And—," Ash swallowed, a trace of resentment underscoring his voice, "—and you kept your distance after that. I thought I'd become a burden to you." He bit his lower lip. "I thought—I thought you couldn't wait to get rid of me."

Luke dropped his head and groaned.

"Shit. I'm so sorry, Ash."

Luke folded his arms around Ash and hugged him carefully, as if he was the most precious thing in the world. He burrowed his face in Ash's hair and pressed a hot kiss to his scalp. "I—I never meant to make you think that. I just needed to keep you away. It was the only way I could protect you from myself."

Ash's pulse thrummed wildly as he listened to Luke's heart pound under his ear, the heat radiating off Luke's hard body so good that Ash almost groaned. He blinked when he finally registered Luke's latest words. Hope bloomed inside Ash, wild and unfettered.

Does he mean what I think he—

"Oh!" Heat flooded Ash's cheeks when he felt Luke's erection dig into his belly. "Um—"

"Fuck." Luke stepped back, an awkward grimace twisting his lips. "I'm sorry!" He turned and rubbed a hand across the back of his neck, but not before Ash caught sight of the thick shape denting the front of his sweatpants.

Understanding finally dawned, the pieces of the puzzle all slotting into place.

Ash blinked rapidly, stunned beyond words.

Jesus, how could I have been so blind?

Luke's cold behavior. The distance he'd deliberately created between them. The length he'd gone to save Ash from harm and to keep him safe all these years.

"Luke." Ash stopped and swallowed hard, his knees so weak he thought he would fall. "The person you love. Is it—*is it me?!*"

Luke stilled. A strangled sound left his throat. "I—I know, it's disgusting. I—"

Ash moved, the euphoria sweeping through him so great he wondered how he didn't fly to Luke's side. He grabbed Luke's shoulder, spun him around, and rose on his tiptoes to press his mouth to Luke's lips. The amber gaze above him flared, Luke's pupils dilating with shock while his body remained frozen to the floor.

Ash blushed and lowered himself back down to the ground.

"I—I've loved you all my life," he said to the dumbfounded man before him. "I love you, Luke Rutherford," Ash continued, his voice growing more confident. "And I don't mean the way a brother loves his sibling. I've been in love with you since I was thirteen years—"

It was as far as Ash got. Luke grabbed his face in both hands, lowered his head, and took his lips in a blistering kiss.

Ash gasped at the feel of Luke's hard mouth against his. Luke molded his lips to Ash's for a timeless moment, learning their shape and testing their resilience, his amber gaze drilling heatedly into Ash's dazed eyes. Then, he ran his tongue along the plump curves before parting them roughly, forcing his way into Ash's mouth. Electricity surged through Ash and sent his dick throbbing as Luke's tongue found his.

Sweet Je—

Ash moaned and clutched the strong shoulders above him, dizzy with desire and pleasure.

Luke cursed and dropped his hands to Ash's waist. He backed Ash across the kitchen while he continued plundering the hot depths of Ash's mouth, each lash of his thick tongue sending bright light flashing across Ash's brain.

Ash shivered when he felt the cool surface of the fridge against his back. Reality fled in the next instant as Luke moved his hands to Ash's butt. Luke dipped and rolled his hips against Ash's, grinding his dick across Ash's aching cock and up his belly while he pressed him back against the fridge.

Holy shit!

The feel of the rock-hard shaft pushing against his taut flesh almost made Ash come there and then. He raised his hands to Luke's head and speared his fingers in the thick black hair he'd dreamed about touching for so long, body melting against the man he loved.

LUKE SWALLOWED A CURSE AT THE SENSUOUS WAY ASH softened into him.

He still couldn't believe this was happening. That he

was finally holding Ash in his arms. That he was kissing him and Ash was kissing him back just as desperately, his tongue moving shyly against Luke's, as if he didn't have any experience of Frenching.

That Ash loved him.

The last part made Luke groan. He knew Ash might come to regret this one day. That he might fall for someone else. He was only twenty-two after all.

But Luke couldn't bear to let him go right now. Couldn't forsake this opportunity to taste the forbidden fruit before him. Couldn't stop himself from touching and kissing the man he loved.

A mechanical buzz reached Luke's ears dimly through the blood roaring in his head. It was followed by a couple of clinks.

"*Oh!*" Ash wrenched his mouth from Luke's and blinked dazedly.

Luke stared. He chuckled when he realized they'd pressed the ice button, sending cold cubes splashing against Ash's back. He dropped his forehead against Ash's, shoulders shaking with silent laughter.

Ash narrowed his eyes and punched him lightly in the chest. "Not funny." His lips curved in a dazzling smile a heartbeat later.

Luke stepped back and took Ash's left hand. He pressed his lips to the pulse point at Ash's wrist and stared at him hotly as he felt Ash's heartbeat skitter all over the place.

"Shall we move this to the bedroom?" he murmured.

CHAPTER ELEVEN

 light burning in Luke's golden eyes.

Luke tugged on Ash's hand and headed briskly out of the kitchen with him in tow.

Oh God.

Heat flooded Ash's cheeks when Luke led him to the stairs and up to his bedroom, his heart racing so fast he thought he would pass out. Ash had a brief impression of a large masculine space when Luke flicked a lamp on, before his widening gaze found the beautiful rosewood bed dominating the ebony floor—an exact replica of the one in Ash's own bedroom, except Luke's was super king-size.

Luke pulled Ash into his arms and took Ash's mouth in a fiery kiss that scattered his nervous thoughts to the four winds and made his dick throb. Luke backed Ash to the bed, grabbed him by the butt, and lifted him against his chest before kneeling on the mattress. Ash gasped as Luke toppled them both down, his hard frame coming to rest intimately against the length of Ash's body while he continued his sinfully delicious assault on Ash's mouth.

Ash moaned as Luke rolled his hips into him, the breathy sound swallowed by the hungry mouth devouring him, the motion of Luke's tongue mimicking what he very much wanted to do to Ash judging by how hard he was. A shiver of anxiety ran through Ash. His unease deepened when Luke slid his hands under his T-shirt, his fingers trailing lines of fire across Ash's twitching skin.

Luke groaned and broke the kiss. He rose to his knees and straddled Ash, his expression growing feverish as he tugged at the T-shirt and peeled it roughly over Ash's head.

Ash shuddered when Luke tossed the garment to the floor and leaned down to press his lips to his bare chest.

"Um, Luke," Ash managed in a strangled voice as Luke rained kisses down his body.

Fuck.

Ash sucked air between his teeth when Luke flicked his tongue across his lower belly, his eyes almost rolling back in his head at the pleasure that stabbed through him. His apprehension returned when Luke grabbed the waistband of his pajama bottoms and started tugging the material down his hips.

"Luke, listen," Ash started, lifting his head to stare dazedly at the man busy worshipping his body, his hot lips and tongue scant inches from Ash's straining cock.

Luke ignored him, his expression dark with desire.

Shit!

Ash grabbed Luke's face in his hands and blurted out the embarrassing words, knowing if he didn't, Luke would ravish him before he could say the word *virgin.*

"I haven't done this before!"

❦

LUKE FROZE. HIS HEAD SNAPPED UP, HIS HEART lurching against his ribs. The shocking words Ash had just spoken rang in his ears. One look at Ash's flushed face and the way he tugged his lower lip sexily between his teeth while he dropped his gaze somewhere near his navel told Luke everything he needed to know about the sinfully wicked admission he'd made.

Bloody hellfire.

Luke rose until he was on all fours above Ash, his breathing ragged and his cock doing push-ups against his sweatpants.

"Would you care to repeat that?" he breathed.

Ash groaned and pressed his hands to his face. He swallowed convulsively.

"I've—I've never had sex before."

Luke cursed out loud. His gaze roamed Ash from his head all the way to his toes, unable to believe the drop-dead gorgeous young man before him had never given himself to anyone.

Luke had his first sexual experience with a woman when he was fourteen and bedded his first man when he was in college. The fact that he was bisexual wasn't something that bothered him, and he'd slept with both women and men over the last decade and a half.

Ash's confession thrilled Luke like few things could. It also brought about a wave of possessiveness that rocked him to the core. Luke was selfishly, stupidly, insanely happy that he would be the first person to make love to Ash. To touch him and kiss him places he'd never been touched and kissed before. To take his body and make him go wild with pleasure. To watch him come apart beneath him as he climaxed.

"Not even a woman?" Luke whispered.

Ash stiffened and peeked at him between his fingers.

Jealousy speared through Luke.

"Well, I did try with a girl in college once," Ash murmured. "Just to see what it was all about."

"And?" Luke said, trying not to make the words come out grating.

"I—um—," Ash hesitated, his ears flaming, "—I couldn't get hard for her," he finished in a breathless rush.

Thank fucking God for that!

Luke squeezed his eyes shut for a second, unable to quell the relief that rushed through him. He lowered his gaze to the shape of Ash's extremely healthy erection beneath his pajama bottoms.

He most definitely isn't impotent.

"Did she touch you?" Luke said thickly.

Ash inhaled sharply, his widening eyes filling with shocked excitement at Luke's dirty question. He bit his lower lip and nodded wordlessly.

"Where?" Luke groaned.

Ash vacillated, his face flushed with the sweetest mix of lust and embarrassment.

"Here?" Luke asked roughly. He raised a hand and trailed it down Ash's chest, his nails gently raking Ash's left nipple.

Ash twitched and arched his back slightly. He nodded shakily.

Luke moved his hand south. "Here?"

Ash whimpered and shivered when Luke stroked the taut skin of his lower belly. He shook his head.

Luke palmed Ash's cock through his pajama bottoms, his fingers closing around the thick, hot shaft while he bit back the groan of need rising in his throat.

"*Oh!*" Ash's eyes widened, his hips jackknifing reflexively off the bed.

Shit.

Luke couldn't help but stroke Ash's twitching length, each glide of his fingers causing the young man to shudder and thrust erratically in his hand. Luke had never seen anything as bewitching as Ash surrendering to the passion burning through his body.

"Did she touch you here?" Luke said hoarsely.

Ash moaned and twisted his fingers in the bedcovers, his blue gaze darkening as he stared at Luke. He nodded.

Envy shot through Luke. He stopped stroking Ash.

Ash flexed his hips against Luke's fingers, unconsciously seeking his touch, his expression pleading.

"Did you like it?" Luke demanded in a voice he hardly recognized.

Ash shook his head, a violent shudder racing through his body.

"Do you like *this*?" Luke started moving his fingers on Ash's cock again.

Ash cried out and arched off the bed. "*Yes!*"

CHAPTER TWELVE

ASH COULDN'T STOP THE SOUNDS THAT RIPPED FROM HIS throat as Luke gave him a hand job through his pajama bottoms, his entire body shivering and jerking on the bed. He couldn't believe how good Luke's hand felt on his dick or how much more pleasure he derived from Luke's touch compared to his own fingers.

Luke cursed and stopped stroking him a moment later.

A moan of need left Ash's lips. It was strangled in the next instant as Luke tugged on Ash's pajama bottoms and dragged them down his thighs and off his legs, taking his briefs with it and causing his erect dick to spring up in the air. Luke tossed the garments to the floor and closed his hand around Ash's naked cock before the latter could utter a protest.

Sanity fled when Luke started stroking him in earnest. Ash's brain turned to gooey mush as the man he loved pleasured him with his hot, bare palm and fingers. Luke knew precisely how fast to rub him, how much pressure to apply, and exactly where to touch him.

A guttural cry left Ash's lips when Luke's clever thumb rubbed across the sensitive head of his rigid shaft. Red waves swam across his vision as Luke repeated the movement again and again. Tension gathered at the base of Ash's spine and his balls. He whimpered when he recognized the sensation of an impending orgasm.

It was stronger than anything he'd ever experienced before, the feeling so tight and burning it made his hole twitch and half-scared him to death.

"*Luke!*" Ash cried out. He grabbed Luke's wrist, alarmed.

Luke resisted his attempt to stay his hand and moved up Ash's body to take his mouth in the sweetest kiss.

"It's okay, Ash," Luke murmured against his lips, his amber gaze as bright as the sun as he stared heatedly down at Ash. "Come for me."

Ash's breath locked in his throat at the filthy command. His orgasm hit him with his next heartbeat, heat blooming deep inside his tense belly. He arched off the bed, his head bowing backward into the mattress, corded neck straining as savage pulses of pleasure started assaulting his body.

Air left Ash's lips in a hoarse shout, his hands rising to twist in the covers on either side of his head. He cried and chanted Luke's name over and over again as his cock pulsed and throbbed, each jet of hot cum that shot out and hit his belly accompanied by the most intense wave of ecstasy he'd ever felt.

❧

LUKE SHUDDERED AS HE WATCHED ASH CLIMAX BENEATH him, the sight so sinfully erotic he knew he would never forget it for as long as he lived.

The way Ash cried and moaned out Luke's name, the way the muscles in his throat tensed and jumped, the flush of color on his chest, the way he erratically rolled his hips and drove his stiff shaft through Luke's fingers—Luke loved it all.

The urge to take Ash nearly overwhelmed Luke then, the musky scent of the young man's cum an intoxicating drug that made his own cock throb and strain in his pants. Luke wanted to fuck Ash now. Wanted to sink his cock into Ash's tight hole with his very next heartbeat. Wanted to thrust repeatedly inside Ash's body until they both shattered violently with pleasure.

The orgasm, Luke knew, would be the best thing he'd ever experienced in his adult life. But he couldn't. Not yet. Not until he had Ash good and ready. He'd be damned if he made Ash's first sexual experience a painful one.

Luke was suddenly grateful for all the men he'd bedded. He knew exactly what he needed to do to make Ash so wild for him that he'd be begging Luke to take him.

Ash collapsed on the bed, his breathing loud and

uneven, sweat beading his forehead and pearling his upper lip as he shivered with the fading waves of his intense climax.

Luke reached over to the nightstand, grabbed some tissue, and wiped the wetness off Ash's belly. Ash's muscles quivered beneath his touch and a tiny moan escaped his lips. He blinked his eyes open when Luke wadded the sodden mass and cast it in the bin by the bathroom door.

Luke studied Ash's dazed, sultry expression before raking Ash's body with his gaze, trying to decide what he was going to touch and kiss next to drive him to another climax. He glimpsed the small sticky patch he'd missed by Ash's navel, wiped it with the pad of his thumb, and sucked his finger.

Ash's eyes widened, his mouth dropping open. "I can't believe you just did that!" he blurted out.

Luke grinned and licked his lips. "Sweet."

Ash covered his face with his hands, his ears flaming. "Oh God."

Luke chuckled. "I'll be doing much worse before the night is over."

Ash peeked at him between his fingers and groaned at his grin. His breath hitched when he looked down and beheld Luke's straining erection. Ash swallowed, the mixture of desire and apprehension in his heated gaze so arousing Luke knew he'd have to jerk off at least once before he touched Ash again.

"Why don't you make yourself comfortable?" Luke said, indicating the head of the bed and the pillows stacked there.

Ash rose up onto his elbows and scooted up the mattress while Luke stepped off and undressed. He yanked his T-shirt over his head, tugged his sweatpants and briefs down, and dropped his clothes onto the messy pile on the floor.

Luke looked up at Ash's sharp inhale. He swallowed a groan at the enraptured expression pasted across Ash's flushed face as he stared, wide-eyed, at Luke's impressive erection.

"Scared?" Luke murmured, his cock throbbing under Ash's heated gaze.

Ash hesitated before shaking his head.

Luke paused, not entirely convinced by Ash's brave expression.

"Maybe we should do this in stages. We don't have to have penetrative—"

Ash's head snapped up, his gaze rising to meet Luke's sharply. Fire flashed in the steel-blue eyes.

"Don't you dare, Luke Rutherford!" he hissed. "We're gonna—," he paused and swallowed, "—we're gonna have sex, and that's that, got it?"

Luke blinked at Ash's sweetly furious words and scowl. He chuckled, climbed back on the bed, and settled on his knees a foot from Ash. He palmed his aching cock with his left hand and started stroking himself.

"Just sit there and watch," Luke said huskily.

CHAPTER THIRTEEN

Ash stared, his heart rising in his mouth.

If he thought being naked and having Luke give him a hand job and watch him orgasm was embarrassing, he obviously hadn't been aware of the other sinfully filthy things Luke had in mind for them. Ash couldn't stop his gaze from roaming over Luke's hard body—from his magnificent broad shoulders and his sculptured six-pack, to his washboard stomach and muscular limbs.

Ash's gaze returned to the part of Luke's anatomy that held his interest the most. He swallowed as he watched Luke slowly rub his own dick. Luke's shaft was thick and veiny, the color flushed and the skin glistening. He wiped at the pre-cum pearling at the broad head and used it as lube as he worked his cock.

Ash's pulse stuttered when Luke exhaled raggedly and started rolling his hips, pumping his dick through his slick hand, his gaze locked on Ash's.

Fuck.

Ash moved, unable to stop himself from getting closer to Luke. He knelt in front of him and reached out with a trembling hand.

Luke hissed and cursed when Ash's fingers landed on his throbbing shaft. He stilled his own hand's stroking motion.

Ash let out a breathy sound, his dick twitching at the amazing feel of Luke's bare cock against his skin. He was hotter and harder than he'd thought he would be. Ash licked his lips and started exploring Luke's thick shaft, bringing his other hand into play.

LUKE BIT BACK ANOTHER SAVAGE CURSE AT THE HEADY feel of Ash's fingers on his dick.

Shit!

He let go and sat back, allowing Ash to investigate his length and thickness. The small jolts of electricity that shot through Luke's cock with each shy stroke of Ash's hands had him gritting his teeth.

"Tell me," Ash whispered.

Luke met Ash's heated blue gaze and blinked, not sure what he was asking.

Ash squeezed Luke's shaft lightly as he started stroking him, causing Luke's hips to jerk.

"Tell me how you like it."

Luke's brain froze for a moment as he stared at Ash. He couldn't believe the man who'd been blushing minutes ago when Luke tasted his cum was asking him such a brazen question. A thrill darted through him.

It looked like Ash would be a wickedly sensual lover.

"Tighter," Luke said hoarsely, his excitement building.

Ash complied eagerly, his fingers clamping around Luke's straining shaft. Luke winced.

"Sorry!" Ash blurted.

Despite the sweet torture Ash was inflicting on his dick, Luke couldn't help the silent laughter that shook him at Ash's contrite expression. He leaned forward and dropped his forehead against Ash's as the latter lightened his grip on Luke's shaft.

"Yeah, just like that," Luke whispered, his eyes on Ash's.

Ash flushed and started stroking him, staring back unblinkingly.

"Faster," Luke hissed, pleasure tightening his balls.

Ash obeyed, his lips parting on ragged breaths as he accelerated the pace of his hands, his steel-blue gaze bright with arousal.

"Touch the tip," Luke groaned.

He lowered his head to the crook of Ash's shoulder, unable to meet Ash's stare any longer. He knew he would come instantly if he carried on looking into Ash's expressive eyes.

"Like this?" Ash whispered, his hot breath washing across Luke's left ear, causing him to shudder.

Luke almost came at the light flick of Ash's thumb across the sensitive head of his rigid cock.

"Jesus, yes!" he bit out.

He flexed and rolled his hips, driving his shaft

through Ash's slick fingers. Tension coiled through Luke's lower back and thighs, his balls and belly so hard and tight he knew his orgasm was seconds away.

"So good, Ash!" Luke said hoarsely.

He leaned back and twisted his hands in the bedcovers, his gaze dropping to where Ash was rubbing him deliciously.

Whiteness filled Luke's mind when his climax washed over him in fierce waves a moment later. He dropped his head back and grunted, hips pumping his throbbing shaft in Ash's hands as pleasure pulsed through him.

⁂

ASH STARED UNBLINKINGLY AT LUKE AS THE LATTER climaxed violently before him, his heart racing in his chest.

He couldn't believe how powerful and beautiful the man he loved looked as he rode his orgasm. The sight of Luke's corded neck and pleasure-dazed face, the way his gorgeous body tensed and trembled with each strong pulse of his shaft, the guttural sounds he made— all of it branded itself in Ash's mind.

A final shudder coursed through Luke seconds later. He relaxed back down onto the bed, his ragged breathing echoing across the bedroom, sweat rolling down his face.

Ash looked at the warm, sticky mess in his hands, Luke's potent scent causing his own dick to throb and swell painfully. He licked his thumb and moaned at the salty, sweet taste of Luke's cum.

Luke groaned, his expression tortured. "Are you trying to kill me?"

He cleaned Ash's hands with tissue and dropped the wet wad of paper on the floor before pushing him down onto the bed. He settled his hard frame against Ash and took his lips in a hot kiss.

Ash shivered as Luke's tongue probed his mouth, heady at the exquisite feel of Luke's weight pressing down on him. He met Luke's masterful strokes with his own tongue, mimicking what Luke was doing to him. Luke evidently approved as he groaned again and cradled Ash's face in his powerful hands, angling Ash's head to take his mouth better.

Ash moaned and gripped Luke's shoulders tightly while the latter ravaged his mouth. Luke moved his lips to Ash's right ear. He licked the shell, his heated breath sending tingles down Ash's spine. He sucked and laved his lobe before suddenly biting down, his teeth tugging on the sensitive flesh.

Ash gasped, his cock throbbing at the delicious sting.

Luke looked up. "Like that?"

Ash nodded and hummed.

Luke's lips curved in a devastating smile. "Good."

Ash shivered when Luke did the same thing to his left ear, his hips flexing reflexively off the bed. He flushed as his cock poked Luke's hard belly.

Luke didn't seem to notice, his attention focused on driving Ash insane with pleasure. He nudged Ash's chin up and kissed his throat, his clever teeth nipping at Ash's skin in delectable bites before he soothed them with his lips and tongue. Ash shivered, his stomach clenching.

Shit.

When Luke moved his attention to Ash's chest, his fingers gently massaging and stroking Ash's firm flesh before his lips and tongue followed his hands' wicked path, Ash knew it wouldn't be long before he climaxed again. He could feel another orgasm slowly building in his lower body, where his cock throbbed and leaked pre-cum against his and Luke's bellies. He dug his fingers into Luke's back and clung to him, nervous and eager to experience that devastating pleasure all over again.

CHAPTER FOURTEEN

"Luke!"

Ash arched when Luke suddenly rubbed his nipples between his fingers and thumbs. Pleasure shot to Ash's dick and hole, causing both to twitch and spasm while Luke twisted and tugged at the delicate, hard nubs. Ash nearly screamed when Luke closed his mouth on his left nipple. Luke kissed, sucked, laved, and bit his sensitive flesh while Ash went wild beneath him, nails raking Luke's shoulders and upper back.

Ash stiffened a second later as he came violently, the swiftness and intensity of his orgasm shocking him. His hips lifted off the bed, his spine bowing while he opened his mouth on a silent cry, too stunned to even breathe at the violent tension gripping him from head to toe.

Incoherent sounds left Ash's throat a heartbeat later as his cock pulsed and jetted out cum between his and Luke's bodies, blinding pleasure filling his mind. Luke ceased torturing Ash's nipple and dropped feathery kisses on Ash's chest as Ash convulsed and shook beneath him.

&a.

LUKE'S BLOOD ROARED IN HIS SKULL, HIS COCK straining and poking Ash's thigh while the latter shuddered and moaned below him, hands digging sweetly into Luke's shoulders. He couldn't help staring at Ash's pleasure-glazed face. He would never tire of this. Of seeing Ash come apart in his arms.

Luke moved down Ash's body, kissing and nipping at his six-pack and his quivering belly.

Ash gasped when Luke nudged his thighs apart and settled between his legs. He lifted his head off the pillow and blinked dazedly along the length of his body at Luke. Luke stuck his tongue out and deliberately licked the sticky cum off Ash's hot, trembling skin, his eyes locked on Ash's steel-blue gaze.

Ash shivered and tugged his lower lip between his teeth. He moved his hands to Luke's head and pushed him down his body.

Luke smiled at Ash's silent, dirty request. He shifted on the bed, curled his hands under Ash's thighs, and pushed them apart and up.

Ash moaned as Luke spread him wide and hooked his knees over his shoulders, Ash's heels coming to rest on either side of Luke's spine.

Luke paused for a moment and stared at the feast laid out before him, his breathing fast and uneven.

Ash's athletic body opened intimately for him, his

flushed cock glistening inches below Luke's face, his trembling sac wet with cum, the shadowy cleft beneath it tantalizingly exposed.

It was all too much.

Luke groaned, opened his mouth, and took Ash inside.

HOLY FU—

Ash cried out as his aching dick was swallowed by Luke's hot, hungry lips.

Pleasure melted his brain as Luke started sucking on his hardening length, his powerful jaw contracting rhythmically while his tongue swirled around the head and lashed his shaft. The feeling was the most arousing, filthiest thing Ash had ever experienced.

He lifted his head off the pillow again and nearly passed out at the sight of Luke's head bobbing up and down his cock. Luke's lashes fluttered against his flushed cheeks, his expression focused as he concentrated on pleasuring Ash.

Ash curled his fingers in Luke's hair and flexed his hips. He grunted as the tip of his cock hit the back of Luke's throat. Luke groaned and swallowed him to the hilt, fingers biting into Ash's thighs while he continued sucking him.

The pleasure spearing Ash was so intense, he thought he was going to have a heart attack. He gripped Luke's hair and finally gave in to his body's natural instinct, thrusting his hips off the bed and fucking Luke's mouth with his cock, hoarse gasps and moans ripped from deep inside him.

Ash's hole twitched and contracted as another orgasm spiraled through his belly and his lower back, tightening his balls and his shaft.

"Luke!"

Ash tugged blindly at Luke's head, trying to get him off.

Luke resisted and flexed his jaw around Ash's cock in two powerful contractions that sent him over the edge.

Ash thrashed his head on the pillow as he came, spine bowing and thighs pressing against Luke's powerful hands where he held him open, his orgasm so savage that black spots swarmed his vision.

Luke continued working his dick with his mouth, his low grunts making Ash's cock quiver while he pulsed and spurted his cum deep inside Luke's throat. Luke swallowed and gently sucked him, his clever lips milking him to the very end.

Ash finally collapsed on the bed, ears buzzing and heart racing, his body drenched in sweat. He didn't think he could take any more of this insane ecstasy.

Luke let go of Ash's cock and moved up his body to kiss him. Ash shivered at the taste of his own cum on Luke's tongue. He blinked his eyes slowly open and gazed into a hot, golden stare.

"We're not done yet," Luke whispered against his lips.

Ash groaned. *I'm going to die.*

Luke bit back a curse at Ash's glassy expression and his swollen, wet lips. He had the sexy, sultry look of a man who had been thoroughly fucked.

Except we haven't quite done that yet.

Luke moved, opened the nightstand drawer, and took out a bottle of lube and a box of condoms.

Ash rose up onto his elbows, interest dawning in his eyes. He frowned a second later.

"Do I even want to know why those look like they've been used?"

Luke grinned. "Well, I'm not exactly a monk."

Ash pouted, causing Luke to chuckle. He leaned over Ash and brought his lips to Ash's right ear.

"Since I turned thirty, I've thought of you every single time I've sunk my cock into another person's body," he whispered, "wishing it was your hole I was fucking." Ash shivered, his cheeks flaming at Luke's erotic words. "Want me to show you what I've always wanted to do to you, Ash?" Luke said, tongue darting out to lick the shell of Ash's ear.

Ash moaned and nodded, his fingers rising to grip Luke's shoulders.

Luke held Ash's chin and kissed him deeply before pushing him down to the bed. He grabbed a pair of pillows, placed them next to Ash's left hip, and rolled him onto them.

CHAPTER FIFTEEN

ASH INHALED SHARPLY WHEN HE FOUND HIMSELF FACE down on the mattress and ass propped up in the air. He rose onto his elbows and looked over his shoulder, his anxious expression tugging at Luke's heart.

"Luke?"

Luke moved up Ash's body and placed a hand on his nape, gently pushing him back down.

"Trust me, Ash," he said huskily, dropping a kiss on the back of his neck. "This is gonna be so good, you'll beg me to do it every time we have sex."

Ash bit his lip. He hesitated before dropping his head forward on the bed, the trust in his eyes so adorable it made Luke's heart melt. Shivers racked Ash's body as Luke pressed hot kisses down his spine.

He stiffened when Luke pushed his legs open and knelt behind him.

Luke swallowed as he stared at the plump, perfect globes of Ash's butt. He caressed and massaged the firm muscles for a moment, causing Ash to twitch as he tested their resilience.

Luke groaned and brought his head down, unable to resist kissing and biting into the beautiful cheeks.

"*Oh!*" Ash arched up into him.

Luke nibbled on Ash's flesh and slowly worked his fingers toward his cleft before gently parting his ass cheeks. He froze when he finally exposed Ash's entrance.

It was as hot and sexy as Luke had imagined it would be, the pink folds meeting together to form the sweetest pucker he'd ever seen.

ASH WENT STILL WHEN HE FELT LUKE'S HOT BREATH wash across his hole. He curled his fingers into the sheets on either side of his head and closed his eyes, a quiver of excitement running through him when he realized what Luke intended to do.

Ash knew of rimming but had never seen it in context to himself.

That Luke was kneeling behind him, exposing his opening and preparing to do just this, was so filthily erotic that Ash couldn't help the sultry moan that left his lips.

Luke repeatedly blew air around and over his hole, making him jerk and pant for breathless seconds. The sudden bite of Luke's fingers in Ash's taut butt cheeks was all the warning Ash got.

"Luke!"

A hot bolt of pleasure shot through Ash's entire body as Luke flicked his tongue against his hole.

"Oh! Oh God!"

Ash couldn't control his cries as Luke started licking him in earnest.

When Luke brought his lips into play and proceeded to kiss and suck his opening, Ash burrowed his face in the mattress and flexed his hips, driving his aching dick into the pillows beneath him while he moaned.

He stiffened when Luke reached between his legs and palmed his throbbing cock.

"Luke! I—I can't! This is too—"

Luke ignored Ash's incoherent cries and continued torturing his quivering hole with his mouth while he stroked his shaft. A familiar tightness gathered at the base of Ash's spine and pooled deep inside his belly, his balls tensing and rising in their sac.

Ash came a moment later, his body writhing and convulsing against the bed as he pumped his cock in Luke's eager hand, soaking his fingers with his hot cum. His breath locked in his throat when he felt his entrance suddenly contract before relaxing and opening.

Luke groaned and dipped his stiff tongue inside, fingers still milking Ash's shaft.

A strangled sob ripped out of Ash. He fisted his hands in the sheets and whimpered, the electric tingles shooting through him as Luke worked his wicked tongue around his tight entrance unlike anything he'd ever felt before.

It was hot. It was dirty. It was indecent. It was also obscenely, crazily good. Luke was right; Ash absolutely, positively loved this.

He surrendered to Luke's sweet torture, the ripples of his fading orgasm gathering in strength once more as he neared another climax. He cried out and chanted Luke's name when he came again, his toes curling with the intense pleasure of it all.

⁂

LUKE STRAIGHTENED, HIS BREATHING RAGGED. HE rolled Ash onto his back and positioned the pillows under Ash's ass.

Rimming and stroking Ash to two successive orgasms had gotten Luke's dick so hard, it bordered on painful.

Luke grabbed a condom from the box on the nightstand, tore the foil, and rolled the latex onto his aching, sensitive cock. He took the lube next and poured a generous amount of the cool liquid onto one hand before briskly working the slick puddle onto his gloved dick and his fingers.

Ash blinked and looked at him woozily when Luke moved inside the cradle of his thighs. Steel-blue eyes flared when they landed on Luke's sheathed, rigid shaft. Ash gasped as Luke grabbed the backs of his calves and guided his legs around his waist.

"Luke," Ash breathed.

Luke stilled, his heart stuttering at the erotic picture Ash made beneath him. Ash's eyes were dark with passion, his swollen lips parted on heated pants, his body limp and trusting. When Ash reached down to grip the inside of his own thighs and pull them apart, Luke's heart almost stopped.

Holy. Fuck.

Luke had never seen anything as sexy and as arousing as Ash sweetly opening himself up for his possession. He clenched his jaw, pushed down on Ash's right thigh, and brought his lubed fingers to Ash's hole.

Ash stiffened, his pupils widening.

Luke stroked and gently played with the soft folds jumping and spasming against his touch. When they contracted and parted a moment later, he dipped the tip of one finger inside.

OH. MY. GOD.

Ash dropped his head back and stared blindly at the ceiling, stunned at the penetration. He'd fingered himself before when he'd jerked off to Luke and had found the experience not too unpleasant.

This was different.

Ash didn't know whether it was because Luke was touching him, or because he was more aroused than he'd ever been in his life, or because he'd just had several orgasms, or because he had just been expertly rimmed. The only thing Ash knew was that his opening had never felt as exquisitely sensitive as it did right now. Even the slightest pressure seemed to cause a dazzling tingle of pleasure that sent white light dancing across his vision.

Ash inhaled sharply when Luke suddenly closed his slick fingers around his cock. He looked down the length of his body and met Luke's golden stare. Ash's breath stuttered when he found himself unable to look away.

Luke steadily stroked Ash's shaft, his hand working its magic once more. Ash bit his lip as his hips lifted off the pillows, his body dancing instinctively to the tune Luke was setting. His hole twitched and contracted around Luke's finger.

"Hmm!" Ash hummed at the hot stab of electricity. His eyes widened and his cheeks warmed when he felt his entrance swallow Luke.

Luke grunted, his gaze still locked on Ash's as he slid his finger deeper inside him. He did something then, something that sent sparks flashing across Ash's mind.

"Luke!" Ash dug his heels in Luke's back and reached down between his thighs to grab Luke's wrist, scared by the shock of intense pleasure.

"That's your prostate," Luke said hoarsely, resisting Ash's attempt to remove his probing digit from his ass while he continued stroking Ash's cock.

Luke curled his finger inside Ash, causing him to cry out as another burst of insane pleasure shot through him. Ash felt his hole spasm and open. He moaned when Luke slipped a second lubed finger inside him, stretching him oh-so deliciously.

The first sensuous waves of Ash's next orgasm tightened his balls and belly before gathering at the base of his spine.

CHAPTER SIXTEEN

LUKE LEANED OVER ASH AND TOOK HIS MOUTH IN A
searing kiss, his gaze locked on the steel-blue one
beneath him as he continued working Ash's rigid shaft
with one hand.

"It's your sweet spot, Ash."

Luke withdrew his slick fingers all the way to the
tips before sliding them back inside, probing the
sensitive area again and causing Ash to curse. He
grunted at the incredible sensation of Ash's hot passage
squeezing and clenching around him.

Fuck, I want to be inside him so bad!

Luke clamped down on the violent urge to take Ash
there and then.

"That's just my fingers." Luke moved his mouth to
Ash's left earlobe and tugged at it with his teeth, a
groan leaving him when Ash's hole spasmed at the sexy
play. "Just imagine how good you're gonna feel when
my—," he dipped his fingers out and thrust them back
in, causing Ash to shout his name, "—thick cock—," he

repeated the movement and swallowed Ash's guttural cry with his lips, "—pounds your prostate."

Ash climaxed savagely, his nails raking Luke's shoulders and his heels digging sharply into Luke's lower back. He lifted his head off the pillow and dropped his chin on his chest, sweat rolling down his flushed face, his spine bowing beautifully, his hips erratically thrusting his pulsing dick into Luke's hand, his opening squeezing and sucking at Luke's invading fingers.

Luke let go of Ash's trembling cock and gripped Ash's right thigh, pushing him open again while he continued working his hole, his heart thundering against his ribs. He grabbed the bottle of lube and poured the liquid directly on Ash's twitching, spasming hole, making him wetter, readying him for his penetration. Luke didn't stop playing with Ash's ass until he brought him to another screaming orgasm. Only then did he pull his fingers out of Ash's trembling body.

Ash collapsed on the bed, eyes closed and sweat-slicked locks plastered to his forehead, his chest heaving with his pants. He shivered when Luke grabbed his hips and tugged him closer.

Luke braced his hands on either side of Ash's head.

Ash blinked his eyes open. His pupils flared when Luke moved up and over him, sheathed cock coming to rest perfectly against his opening.

"Can you feel me, Ash?" Luke growled, stroking the tip of his cock up and down Ash's quivering entrance, knowing he was more than ready for this.

Ash followed Luke's gaze to the delicious sight of their bodies about to become one. He moaned and tugged his lower lip between his teeth, his belly trembling in anticipation.

"Do you want me, Ash?" Luke bit out, raring to go but keeping himself in check by the thinnest of threads.

Ash nodded shakily and reached up to grip Luke's shoulders.

Luke stilled. "Say it, Ash."

Luke swooped and took Ash's mouth in a deep kiss before straightening.

Ash flushed beneath him, blue eyes pleading. "Luke," he whispered.

Luke swallowed a groan. "Yes, Ash?"

Ash rolled his hips and rubbed his hole against Luke's dick.

"I want you inside me," he whimpered. "Please!"

❧

ASH'S BREATH FROZE IN HIS LUNGS WHEN LUKE NUDGED his hips forward.

"*Oh!*"

The broad head of Luke's cock pushed against his trembling hole, sweetly parting him, spreading him open.

Luke's pupils dilated above him, golden eyes flaring with pleasure.

"So good," he growled. "So fucking good, Ash!"

Ash blushed. He widened his eyes as Luke moved his hips again, driving his cock further inside. Ash's hole stung and burned as Luke's thick shaft stretched the tight rings of muscles guarding the inside of his entrance.

Luke stilled above him. "You okay?"

Ash bit his lip and nodded shakily, too stunned to speak at the incredible sensation of Luke's penetration. The soreness was already fading.

"It doesn't hurt?" Luke said, concern furrowing his brow. He pushed his hips against Ash's.

Ash gasped as Luke slid past the tight rings and glided in effortlessly, opening him up more.

"Luke!"

Luke gritted his teeth and flexed his hips.

"Oh God!" Ash cried out as Luke slid all the way home to the hilt, his sac coming to rest against Ash's butt cheeks.

"I'll take that as a no," Luke groaned.

He dipped his head and kissed Ash hotly, his tongue sweeping roughly inside Ash's mouth.

Ash gasped as Luke slowly rolled his hips, his thick shaft dipping smoothly out of Ash's tight, wet hole before sliding back in. Tingles jolted through Ash from deep inside his spasming passage, the hot friction and feel of Luke repeatedly thrusting his cock into his body so erotic he could only moan and blush.

That was, until Luke grabbed his left hip and angled him up slightly.

Lightning exploded inside Ash's mind. He cried out as the most intense, searing pleasure he'd ever known bloomed deep inside him and rippled through his body.

Luke swallowed the sound, his tongue mimicking the motion of his body as he stabbed and plundered Ash's mouth as masterfully as he was fucking him.

Awareness fled as wave after wave of fierce sensation washed through Ash, the broad head of Luke's thick cock finding the sweet spot inside him over and over again—massaging it, nudging it, prodding it. Ash climaxed once, twice, three times as Luke continued plunging inside his body, dimly aware that he was having one dry orgasm after another.

Luke dropped his head in the crook of Ash's neck as he accelerated his pace, his hips flexing deeply, his ragged breathing and grunts a sweet symphony that matched Ash's breathless, incoherent cries and moans.

Ash felt a savage pressure build inside his belly. He hiccuped, his nails raking Luke's back while his thighs rose instinctively higher, opening himself more widely and deepening Luke's penetration.

Luke swore and started pumping his hips harder, driving Ash into the bed and causing red waves of ecstasy to pulse across Ash's vision. Ash let out a long, guttural shout as the overpowering climax finally swept over him, his toes curling, his back bowing off the bed.

Luke bit Ash's shoulder as he came violently, his cock swelling and pulsing deep inside Ash, his hips jackknifing erratically against Ash's spasming passage, his harsh breaths panting out of his nose. His thrusts slowed as they rode the final waves of their orgasms together, deep shudders racking their bodies.

Luke raised his head and took Ash's mouth in the sweetest kiss.

They sagged on the bed, Luke's weight on Ash so delicious he couldn't help but sigh in contentment. The sound turned to a gasp when Luke wrapped his arms around him and rolled off the pillows and onto his back, Ash coming to rest on top of him.

Ash shivered as the motion shifted Luke's cock inside him.

Luke lovingly wiped a sweat-slicked lock from Ash's forehead and pressed a kiss to the tip of his nose.

"You okay?"

Ash could only nod, the fading pulses of potent pleasure still echoing through his mind and body.

A wickedly filthy smile curved Luke's lips.

"So, Mr. Colby, how does it feel to have your cherry finally popped?"

Heat flooded Ash's cheeks at Luke's teasing tone. "It was fucking awesome," he murmured.

Luke grinned. "Only awesome?"

Ash inhaled shakily. "It was breathtaking."

Luke chuckled. "*Really?*"

"Magnificent," Ash said, warming to their game.

"Uh-huh?"

"Formidable."

Luke flexed his hips slightly.

Ash gasped when he felt Luke swell and harden inside him.

"I'm sure you can do better," Luke teased, fingers moving to massage Ash's butt cheeks.

Ash groaned and cradled Luke's face in his hands.

"Your dick should be made a wonder of the world. There, happy?" he said with fake sternness.

Luke laughed out loud and kissed him.

Ash moaned when Luke pulled his stiff cock out of him and sat them both up. He blinked, surprised. He bit his lip and stared as Luke stripped the cum-filled condom off his rock-hard shaft and discarded it.

Luke paused and looked at him, his golden gaze full of love.

"Don't worry." He grabbed Ash's hand, climbed off the bed, and tugged him toward the bathroom. "We're only moving things to another location."

"Oh." Ash's gaze moved to the large, black marble and glass shower. He flushed as he imagined all the wicked things they could do together under the pounding water.

"I think you'll be saying more than *oh* by the time morning comes," Luke said with a sexy smile.

He dropped a kiss on Ash's head and slapped his butt lightly as he urged him into the shower.

Oh.

CHAPTER SEVENTEEN

ASH SIGHED AND BURIED HIS FACE IN THE FIRM, WARM pillow beneath his head. A gentle touch danced across his cheek a moment later. He smiled, content, and arched instinctively into it.

"Morning, sleepyhead."

Ash blinked, the husky voice sending a hot tingle down his spine. He looked up and met Luke's amber stare. Heat flooded his face when he realized he was draped wantonly across Luke, his head on Luke's chest and his right leg and arm flung casually across Luke's hard body.

Ash made to move. Luke tightened the arm resting around Ash's waist.

"Stay," Luke murmured. He pressed a kiss to Ash's forehead. "I love the way you curl up to me when you sleep."

Ash blushed and relaxed back down on Luke, happiness filling him while he listened to the steady beat of the strong heart beneath his ear. He shifted his legs and winced slightly at his sore hips and pleasantly aching hole.

Even though Ash had been a virgin, Luke had shown him little mercy last night, taking him and claiming him in all kinds of sinfully wicked positions in the shower and back on the bed. Ash flushed as he recalled the way Luke had taught him how to ride his cock cowboy-style, and how Luke had him kneel on the edge of the bed before standing and taking him from behind, his thrusts so powerful he had to anchor Ash's hips in place with his hands while Ash practically screamed from the fierce pleasure of his forceful possession.

Ash had lost count of the number of dry orgasms and ejaculations Luke had brought him to by the time he wrapped his arms around him and they fell asleep.

Luke's cell suddenly rang in the comfortable silence around them. He sighed.

"That's probably John, wondering where the hell I am."

"What time is it?" Ash mumbled as Luke reached for his phone on the nightstand.

"Ten."

Ash stiffened and clambered to his knees. "Shit! Isn't Xin here?"

"She probably is," Luke said with a faint smile. "The door's closed and my bag's still in the hallway. She won't disturb us."

A puzzled expression flashed in Luke's eyes as he

stared at the screen of his cell. He touched the answer button and brought it to his ear.

"Who is this?"

Ash blinked when Luke went deathly still beside him. One look at the anger igniting his amber eyes and Ash instinctively knew who was on the end of the line.

"What the hell do you want, Catherine?" Luke ground out, confirming Ash's suspicions. "And how the fuck did you get this number?"

Ash's mouth went dry as he stared at Luke, apprehension twisting his stomach.

Luke frowned and listened, a muscle jumping in his jawline.

"Would you care to repeat that?" he said silkily.

Fury suddenly surged through Ash, erasing his fear. After all the misery Catherine and Peter Bernardino had visited on Luke and him, that they'd even dare try to hurt them again was something Ash could no longer abide.

He grabbed the phone from Luke and pressed the speaker button.

"...you don't send us five million, I'll make sure everyone knows the heir of Rutherford Industries wanted to rape a minor all those years back," Catherine grated out across the connection. "How's that nephew of mine these days? Have you drilled his hole yet?"

"Hello, Catherine," Ash hissed.

Luke made to take the phone from him. Ash shook his head and stayed his hand. He linked his fingers through Luke's, glad for their solid strength and warmth.

Silence descended on the line.

"Luke told me everything about what happened back then, so there's no need for you to lie," Ash said in a hard voice. "Let me make one thing abundantly clear. You and Peter are never going to get a single cent off Luke or the Colby Trust again, so whatever it is you're up to, you had better—"

"You little shit!" Catherine barked. "Don't you dare speak to me like that!"

The dial tone suddenly sounded.

Ash blinked and stared at the cell. "Well, that ended faster than I thought it would."

He looked up.

Luke was gazing at him with a wide-eyed expression. Ash gasped when Luke suddenly grabbed his face and kissed him.

"You're a genius!" Luke said fiercely.

He took the phone, tapped the touch screen, and pulled up another number.

Ash studied him, bemused, as the line rang.

"Where are you?" John Peace barked when it connected. "I have the president of Keele Industries on the other line, and she's—"

"Good morning to you too, sunshine," Luke interrupted with a grin. "I'm in bed. With Ash."

Ash blushed as silence resonated across the connection.

John sighed. "I said, talk to him, not fuck him," he muttered. "Anyway, it looks like congratulations are in order. I hope the kid can walk."

"John," Luke said, stifling a chuckle while Ash's ears flamed.

"Yeah?"

"You're on speaker."

There was a brief pause.

"Good morning, Ash," John said, unperturbed.

Ash groaned and covered his face with his free hand.

"'Morning, John," he mumbled.

"Guess who just phoned?" Luke said to John.

Ash didn't bother hiding his puzzlement at the triumphant expression in Luke's golden eyes.

"Really?" John said sarcastically. "You want me to play a guessing game? You're the CEO of Rutherford Industries. I've got, like, a gazillion people on your contacts list."

"Well, one of them probably spilled my private number to Catherine Bernardino," Luke responded drily.

"She called you?" John snapped. "What did she say?" He swore. "Did that bitch threaten you again?"

Luke smiled.

"It wasn't so much *what* she said but rather *who* she said it to. Remember Clause One B of the contract I showed you on Monday? The one the Bernardinos signed five years ago?"

John's sharp inhale traveled down the line.

"You mean about the permanent injunction order?" he said excitedly. "The one that states they are not allowed to communicate with Ash by any means or get within a mile of him?"

"Yup, that one." Luke leaned in and dropped a loving kiss on Ash's forehead. "Ash grabbed my phone off me. Catherine spoke to him. It was only a few words, but I believe my lawyers will ride with that. Phone them and get them to file a petition for contempt. The PI firm in San Francisco should be closing in on the Bernardinos' whereabouts by now. Oh, and, John? I'm taking the day off. Tell Lana Keele something came up and I'll ring her tomorrow."

Ash's pulse raced when Luke ended the call.

"You mean, this could all be over soon?" he breathed.

Luke placed the cell on the nightstand and tugged Ash against his chest as he lay back down on the bed.

"Yup. And all because you lost your temper." He dropped another kiss on the tip of Ash's nose. "Which, let me tell you, is very arousing. I'm kinda hard right now."

Ash flushed when he registered Luke's stiffening length against his hip.

"You sex fiend."

Luke grinned. His smile faltered a moment later.

"Ash, about Stanford. I'm sorry I acted like an ass." He grimaced. "I was just worried about you, so if you wanna go—"

Ash rose and pressed his mouth to Luke's, checking his words. Luke groaned and kissed him hotly, his tongue probing Ash's lips until the latter moaned and let him in. Ash wrenched his mouth from Luke's breathless seconds later.

"I can't believe you'd even suggest that." Ash stared

down at Luke. "I can earn an architectural design degree anywhere, Luke. This is where I want to be. With you. Right here."

Luke's eyes brightened to molten gold, the emotion in the amber depths causing Ash's breath to catch all over again.

"Are you sure?" Luke said thickly.

Ash swallowed, emotion clogging his throat. He pressed a kiss over Luke's heart and rested his head against his chest, the steady drumming beneath his ear a balm that soothed his soul.

"I've never been so sure of anything in my life." Ash took a ragged breath. "Don't send me away again, Luke. I couldn't bear it if you—"

He gasped when Luke suddenly flipped him onto his back.

"I'm never letting you go," Luke growled. He kissed Ash passionately. "You'd better be prepared, Ash Colby."

Ash nodded. He moaned as Luke dropped hot kisses down his neck and across his chest.

"Luke, maybe we should, you know, get up and have breakfast," Ash managed to say in a strangled voice as Luke's clever lips found his left nipple.

"My breakfast is right here," Luke muttered.

He dipped his head and kissed the stirring head of Ash's cock.

Ash flushed. *This beast. I can't believe he's—Oh fuck!*

THE END

Can Ash Colby convince Luke Rutherford that they belong together?

Get Sweet Possession (Nights #5)
Turn the page to read an extract now!

SWEET POSSESSION
(NIGHTS SERIES BOOK 5)
SPECIAL PREVIEW

CHAPTER ONE

LUKE RUTHERFORD LEANED AGAINST THE SLIDING DOOR that opened onto the sun deck and took a sip of his coffee while he watched the man in the pool. His gaze followed the clean lines of Ash Colby's shoulders and his strong, toned back before lingering on the powerful legs scissoring through the water. Legs that had been wrapped around Luke's hips only hours ago when they were making love and that had gripped his body with savage ferocity when Ash came apart beneath him, his hole quivering and clenching hungrily on Luke's dick while he bowed his spine and cried out in mindless pleasure.

Luke still couldn't believe the gorgeous young man cleaving the water so seamlessly twenty feet from where he stood was finally his. Having doted on Ash since the day he was born and been consumed with desire for him for the last six years, Luke had always imagined his forbidden love for the boy who had grown up looking up to him as a brother was doomed from the start.

Furthermore, as Ash's former guardian and the current trustee of the Colby trust fund, Luke had known acting on his carnal urges would blur the boundaries of acceptable behavior, even after Ash turned eighteen and stopped being his ward. Besides, Luke hadn't ever once imagined Ash would even care for him in that way.

That Ash had been in love with him for even longer than he had, had come as a complete shock to Luke.

It wasn't until Luke had forcibly relocated Ash from Stanford to Singapore two months ago that the complicated charade both men had been playing for the last five years finally came crashing down around them. Uprooting Ash from the only life he had ever known in the US was not a decision Luke had taken lightly, the drastic measure having been forced upon him by the actions of Ash's estranged Aunt Catherine Bernardino—the sister of Ash's dead father, Charles Colby.

Half a decade after Luke squashed the beginnings of a deadly plot that could have ended Ash's life and delivered the substantial inheritance locked in the Colby trust fund to his only living relative, Catherine, the woman had had the gall to contact Luke again to blackmail him. Having paid her and her husband off handsomely to get the hell out of Ash's life for good, Luke had not taken kindly to her threat, nor had he been able to control his rage when he discovered the true extent of the damage the woman who had nearly destroyed his and Ash's relationship had caused all those years ago.

It was only Ash's presence that quelled his burning desire to find and physically hurt Catherine that day. Ash's touch that soothed Luke's agonizing pain at the realization that he had inadvertently hurt the person he loved most in this world. Ash's kiss that transformed the storm inside his heart into a maelstrom of passion that had seen Luke take the young man's virginity, finally making him his in every sinful and sacred sense of the word.

It was also Ash who had abruptly ended the nightmare situation Catherine had been trying to create to extract more money from Luke. Having broken the permanent injunction order forbidding the Bernardinos from making any form of contact with Ash, the couple had had a petition for contempt filed against them in California in the last month and were currently facing jail time. Add to this fresh evidence gathered by the PI firm Luke had had keeping an eye out on them showing the fraudulent investments they had made with the money Luke had given them five years ago, and Luke knew he and Ash had finally seen the last of the Bernardinos.

With Ash settling into his new life at the university in Singapore and their relationship coming along in leaps and bounds, Luke had never known such happiness.

His dick stirred as Ash completed his final lap and climbed out of the pool, sunlight dancing on his glistening, honey-colored skin, and toned limbs. Not only was Luke utterly and blissfully content, he had also never been so completely and utterly sexually satisfied.

Luke discovered he had a high sex drive when he was still in his teens and had bedded plenty of women and men over the years to fulfill his formidable carnal needs. Yet the gratification he found in Ash's arms was something new to him. More than the searing pleasure of being inside Ash's body, more than the fierce orgasms they achieved every time they made love, what Luke treasured above all was the sense of completeness he found in Ash's arms. He had never felt so whole in his entire life. It was as if they were two pieces of a puzzle, made for one another from the day they were born and destined to be together for eternity.

The fiery ardor of their first night together had only gotten stronger in the last two months, with Ash as eager to explore his burgeoning sensuality as Luke was keen to teach him. Seeing Ash discover what a sexual being he was had become Luke's new addiction, as was watching the young man climax. It was a craving that had been too long denied, a secret obsession that consumed Luke whenever they breathed the same air.

Ash dried himself with a towel and headed toward him, oblivious to the filthy thoughts crowding Luke's mind. "Morning." He rose on his tiptoes and dropped a chaste peck on Luke's lips, his steel-blue gaze bright. "I thought I'd take an early morning swim before we started our day. What time is John's housewarming party again?"

Luke placed his coffee on the garden table, looped

his arm around Ash's waist, and pulled him in tight before swooping down to take his mouth in a searing kiss. Ash moaned and eagerly parted his lips, letting Luke in. Their tongues clashed deliciously. Ash dropped the towel and gripped Luke's shoulders, his glazed eyes fluttering closed under the sensual assault.

Luke was rock hard by the time he ended the kiss.

"It starts at two," he murmured, his pulse racing erratically.

John Peace, Luke's secretary, had finally given in to his long-suffering partner's wishes and bought a place with him.

"What do you have to do before then?" Ash asked hoarsely, his hips twitching and his erection digging into Luke's left thigh.

Luke swallowed a groan.

You. I want to do you.

Although Luke wanted nothing more than to take the young man in his arms and go straight back to bed to fuck the living daylights out of him, some urgent paperwork needed his attention. Being the head of the billion-dollar Rutherford Industries and the only surviving heir of the Rutherford dynasty meant hardly a day passed when Luke didn't have something to do for work, even on a Sunday. Not that he minded it. He would never have driven Rutherford Industries to the dizzying heights of success they had achieved since he took command of his family business had he not truly been passionate about the job.

Still, Luke always made sure to find time for Ash since he'd moved the young man in with him. Like having dinner together every night even if it meant Ash coming over to his office in Marina Bay and bringing the meals their housekeeper, Xin, prepared for them when Luke was having a late night at work. Or their lazy Sunday mornings when they would have breakfast out on the sun deck and relax in each other's company.

"I need to look over some documents," Luke said reluctantly. "You?"

Ash grimaced.

"I have a couple more hours to do on an assignment due tomorrow." He wrinkled his beautiful nose. "Remember that international architecture and design competition I told you about—the one in Madrid? Well, my supervisor at Stanford and my new professor here entered me into it without telling me first. The deadline is in six weeks. I have to work on that project as well as all my regular coursework."

Luke's heart swelled with pride. He'd always known Ash was incredibly talented. The fact that the people around Ash were acknowledging this in their own way thrilled Luke like few things could.

He dropped a kiss on Ash's forehead and tipped his chin up.

"You can do it. I believe in you."

Ash smiled, his eyes sparkling with happiness. His expression faltered a moment later. "Shit."

"What?" Luke said, tensing up.

Ash tugged his lower lip between his teeth and dropped his gaze to Luke's mouth. "I really wanna have sex right now."

Luke groaned at the sinfully sensuous look on Ash's face. *This kid will be the death of me.*

"Don't," Luke muttered. "I'm only barely holding on myself."

Ash's eyes widened when his gaze dropped to Luke's glorious erection tenting the front of his pajama bottoms. He grinned and ran his index finger along Luke's hard length.

"What a brave trooper."

Luke shuddered, his cock jerking at Ash's teasing touch. "You're playing with fire, Ash," he warned gruffly.

Ash looked up at him, his eyes darkening, his expression utterly unrepentant. "We gave Xin the day off, right?"

Luke nodded, not trusting himself to speak.

Ash's lips curved in a seductive grin. He raised his hands to his hips and took off his swimming trunks.

Luke's pulse spiked as his hot gaze roamed Ash's delectable, naked body and his straining, flushed dick.

Ash arched an eyebrow. "I bet I can halve the time it takes to complete that assignment. Why don't you look over your documents and come find me? I'll be in the bedroom." Ash licked his lips and palmed Luke's cock lightly. "Waiting for you to sink this—," he tugged playfully on Luke's shaft, causing him to groan, "—so deep inside me, I'll see stars."

Ash headed past Luke and gave him a come-hither look over his shoulder as he sashayed into the mansion, the swimming trunks swinging carelessly from his index finger.

Fuck.

Luke vacillated for all of five seconds before following Ash.

His reason fled when he entered the bedroom and found Ash lying on their bed, fingers already working lube into his ass while he stroked his hard dick, his thighs open wide in an unmistakable invitation, his blue eyes dark and sultry with desire.

Luke was inside Ash in less than ten seconds and brought him to his first orgasm in under five minutes.

They barely made it to John's housewarming party.

Read Sweet Possession today

AFTERWORD

To all my friends who helped make this possible. You
know who you are.

To you, my readers. Thank you for reading Ash and
Luke's story. I hope you loved this fourth book in the
Nights series. I would be grateful if you could leave a
review on Goodreads or on the store where you
purchased this book. Reviews help readers like you
find my books and I truly appreciate your honest
opinions about my stories.

Make sure to sign up to my store newsletter for special
deals on my books and new release alerts. Or you can
sign up to my author newsletter instead to get
upcoming release notifications, sneak peeks, and
giveaways.

ABOUT THE AUTHOR

Ava Marie Salinger is the romance pen name of an Amazon bestselling author with a passion for writing addictive tales. Known for her action-packed and thrilling urban fantasy novels, she has expanded her repertoire with the introduction of the M/M urban fantasy romance series Fallen Messengers. Additionally, she has penned the scorching hot contemporary M/M romance series Nights and Twilight Falls as A.M. Salinger. When not immersed in her writing, Ava can be found curating inspiring music playlists, indulging in her love for nature, marveling at the latest gadgets, and savoring Chinese cuisine.

You can find all of Ava's books on her author store at
shop.adstarrling.com